12 Nights Of Christmas

Katie Night

12 Nights of Christmas
Copyright © 2024 by Katie Night

All rights reserved. No part of this book may be reproduced, stored in a retrieval system, or transmitted in any form or by any means—electronic, mechanical, photocopying, recording, or otherwise—without prior written permission from the publisher, except for brief quotations in reviews or articles.

ISBN- 979-8-3485-2113-4

Cover design by Lilith Luxe and Author's Aura
Interior design by Katie Night

This is a work of fiction. Any resemblance to actual persons, living or dead, events, or locations is purely coincidental.

First Edition: December, 2024

Contents

Dedication	VI
Trigger Warnings	VII
1. Her	1
2. Him	7
3. Her	9
4. Him	17
5. Her	20
6. Him	27
7. Her	30
8. Her	39
9. Him	51
10. Her	52
11. Him	65
12. Her	67

13.	Him	74
14.	Her	81
15.	Him	86
16.	Her	88
17.	Him	97
18.	Her	99
19.	His	107
20.	Her	116
21.	Him	122
22.	Her	125
23.	Him	134
24.	Her	136
25.	Him	145
26.	Her	147
27.	Her	153
28.	Him	159
29.	Him	166
30.	Her	174
31.	Him	179
Epilogue		186
Acknowledgements		190
About the author		192

To all the bratty girls who just need a masked man to fuck the attitude out of them.

Trigger Warnings

This book contains scenes that may depict, mention, or discuss: stalking, somnophilia, consensual-Non consent, and verbal degradation.

Her

I do this every damn year. Every year, I tell myself it'll be different. And maybe this time, it would have been; if I hadn't walked in on my boyfriend—well ex-boyfriend—fucking our math tutor.

I had showed up early to our weekly study group; we were meeting to prepare for finals before the holidays. And there she was—on her hands and knees on the coffee table where we ate so many meals together. Her tits were out and bouncing with every thrust as he plowed into her from behind.

The worst part was how hard he came the moment he realized I was standing there. Like the sheer thrill of getting caught was all he needed to find release.

I stood frozen, rooted to the spot, unable to tear my eyes away from the twisted scene unfolding before me. She, at least, had the decency to scramble to cover herself when she noticed me. Before his haze of pure bliss could clear, I turned and bolted.

I force myself not to cry as I weave through the crowds of fellow last-minute Christmas shoppers. At least this time, I have a good reason for procrastinating. I would've had everything done weeks ago if my cheating bastard of an ex hadn't decided to stick his dick where it didn't belong.

And it isn't like I wasn't putting out. I love sex. Okay, maybe not sex with *him*. He was just so vanilla. I always had to wait until he passed out to get myself off, and even then, I always felt like something was missing. Oh, how I long for a man who knows how to *use* me. No matter how many times I told Jake what I wanted—he just couldn't get the job done. No amount of direction worked. So, really, this isn't a loss, is it? Maybe things worked out for the best after all.

With my newfound resolve, I press on, more determined than ever. I still have three people to shop for—four if you count my bestie, Amara. But, this year, we decided to skip the gifts and put our money towards a ski trip for a long weekend instead. At the time, it was mostly Mara who needed to get away after her breakup. Nothing dramatic like what happened with Jackass and me, but still painful. She and her ex boyfriend were high school sweethearts, and now we're seniors in college. They simply grew apart; what they wanted six years ago wasn't what they wished for anymore.

So, we're taking my parents' reservation at the lodge to go skiing. Who am I kidding? Neither of us is coordinated enough for that shit. We're really going for the *view*—and not the mountains either.

My family usually goes every year, but this time, Mom and Dad are out of the country until Christmas Eve. They were absolutely thrilled when I told them their non-refundable package wouldn't go to waste, especially since their spontaneous three-month trip left them scrambling to figure it out.

We leave at the end of the week, so I need to finish my shopping now. At least Dad was easy. I already reached out to the Photoshop he'll use to print some of the pictures he'll take on their trip, and they'll be creating an album for him. He's sentimental like that, so he'll love it. Mom, on the other hand, was trickier. It took some serious thought, but I finally came up with the perfect gift.

I wave to an assistant buyer as I step into the Chanel store. Almost immediately, a thin man dressed to impress approaches me. His tailored three-piece black suit pairs surprisingly well with his bright yellow square-frame glasses. He offers a warm smile as he greets me.

"Welcome. What can I help you with today?"

I return his smile. "Hello! I'm here to pick up a bag I brought in for repair and cleaning."

Dad had gifted Mom a one-of-a-kind vintage bag on their wedding day, and it's been lovingly worn ever since. With their twenty-fifth anniversary vow renewal coming up this spring, I decided to have it restored as a surprise.

"Ah, yes. Right this way." He gestures toward the counter.

When he hands me the clean and perfectly restored bag, I feel a swell of satisfaction. Mom's going to love it. With that checked off my list, I turn my attention to finding something for my brother. Knowing there's nothing here that would work for him—and that I'll probably have to shop online—I make my way to the exit.

On my way home, I stopped for Chinese takeout. There's nothing like a good sesame chicken and fried rice to cap off a long day. Luckily, I don't have to worry about the boys stealing my food tonight—it's Friday, and they'll be out for hours, if they even come home at all.

I live with my brother, and his friends are constantly in and out of the house. Our parents didn't like the idea of us living on campus with "strangers," so they bought us a house just a five-minute walk away. The setup works pretty well: the upstairs is my space, the finished basement is his, and we share the kitchen and living room.

His friends refuse to bring girls around me, and honestly, I can't blame them. I've got a reputation for being a total bitch when it comes to looking out for them. What can I say? Someone has to keep them in line.

All I want to do is change, eat, and curl up with a book on the couch. With that in mind, I set my food on the black granite countertop in the kitchen and head upstairs to my room. I slip into a pair of loose gray shorts and my favorite oversized black T-shirt, then throw my blonde hair up into a messy bun and wash the makeup off my face.

Feeling refreshed, I walk into the spare bedroom I've turned into a library. A couple of days ago, I finished a football romance, but tonight I'm in the mood for something darker. I decide on the first book in a series about a secret society. The premise is deliciously twisted: members spend their college years proving their loyalty through a series of intense trials. The hardest test? Celibacy for the first three years.

But the reward is what really hooked me. After three years of dedication, each member gets to pick a "Chosen"—a woman selected to satisfy his every desire for the rest of the year. The descriptions of how he unleashes himself on her are the kind of dark fantasies I could only dream of.

I'm already halfway through the book, so I grab it and head downstairs to read while I eat. Dinner is as delicious as ever—sesame chicken and fried rice never disappoint. It's one of my favorite meals, and I savor every bite. Jake never cared for it, though. Honestly, after three years together, it's clear he never really understood me at all.

Before I let my thoughts spiral too far, I pack up the leftovers and place them in the fridge. Then I grab my favorite dark green fuzzy blanket and curl up on the couch, settling into my usual spot on the chaise side.

Once I'm comfortable, I pick up my book and dive back in. The hero has just claimed his Chosen, and the scene is everything I've been craving. He takes her roughly, possessively, pressing her up against the side of a building.

It doesn't take long before I feel my pussy growing wet, my nipples hardening into tight peaks as I fantasize about being the girl in the book. The thought of being so deeply desired by a man—so consumed by his need for me—sends a shiver down my spine.

Even more thrilling is his possessiveness, the way he refuses to let anyone else see or touch what's his. When he grabs her throat in the story, my own fingers skim lightly over my neck.

I want that. I want someone to take their pleasure from me, to claim me so completely that it feels like I'm drowning in the intensity of it. I imagine the kind of pleasure that's like pin pricks igniting across my skin, until I finally explode around him.

I can't take it anymore. I haven't been fucked in weeks, and even then, I've never been fucked the way I crave. The way my body *needs* it. But I know myself well enough to recognize that after all this fantasizing, it won't take much to curb that ache, at least for now.

With that thought, I drop my book onto the couch beside me and shove the blanket aside, exposing myself to the cool air. One hand lifts my shirt, baring my breasts, as the other moves my shorts to the side. I start massaging my breast, rolling my nipple until a whimper escapes my lips.

My other hand drifts lower, sliding through the wetness gathered at my opening. I don't bother dipping into my liquid heat—I know I won't cum that way. Instead, I glide my fingers up straight to my clit. The second I make contact, my back arches off the couch, and a heady moan is released from my throat.

I circle my clit, working it faster and harder, chasing that sweet release. My body tightens, every single muscle coiling like a spring, until finally, a wave of pure, unrelenting ecstasy crashes over me.

I keep rubbing, desperate to prolong the pleasure, to let the wave roll over me again until I'm satisfied. But soon, the intensity ebbs, and I'm left stroking myself idly, the craving still gnawing at me.

Him

Standing outside her house, concealed by the shadows, I watch her. Oblivious to the darkness beyond her window, she touches herself. I take note of the way she pinches her nipples, simply moving her shorts to the side, teasing, though I ache to see her pussy. I bet she's soaking wet—tight and needy. Her cries would echo in my ears, her body mine to command. I will claim every inch of her, down to her soul.

The urge to take her consumes me. I bet that piece-of-shit ex of hers never knew what to do with her. Never gave her what she craves, what she *deserves*. My fists clench as I watch her fingertips hover over her swollen clit. She doesn't slip her fingers inside her entrance, but I'm surprised to notice she doesn't cum nearly as hard as she needs to, even with how tightly she is wound up. It's proof enough—she doesn't know how to give herself what she needs.

But I do. She needs *me*.

My cock throbs against the rough fabric of my jeans. I shift, trying to ease the pressure by adjusting my cock, but it only makes the ache worse. The thought of her wet heat clenching around me—tight, perfect—sends my control spiraling. The urge to storm into the house and bury myself as deep inside her as possible overwhelms me. I unbuckle my belt, spit into my palm, and fist my cock.

I think it's time my beautiful little angel learned exactly what she does to me.

Every stroke is a fantasy. Imagining my hand is her tight, wet cunt, squeezing with her climax as I fuck her relentlessly, leaving my mark inside her. Claiming her. The image is so vivid, it doesn't take much for me to blow my load. My vision blurs, my body shudders, and I stumble against the tree for support.

Panting, I peel off my hoodie and tug my shirt over my head, using it to wipe the cum away from my still semi-hard cock. Once clean, I pull the hoodie back on and reach for the small notepad and pen I always keep in my pocket.

I hastily make a note, deciding this is the first gift she will get from me this year.

Her

Last night left me restless, and more sexually frustrated than ever before. Even the thought of using a toy feels pointless.

No matter how hard I try, or how close I get, it's like the moment I should have tipped into ecstasy, something yanks me back. Like riding a rollercoaster, the excitement building until it crests, but the ride stops right at the top, before I can actually fall into oblivion. I've never cum the way other girls talk about—the kind that leaves you shaking, boneless, wrecked. But I want it. I *crave* it. What I need is more than my hands, more than the hollow buzz of silicone.

When I come downstairs, the sight of Damien sprawled out on the couch stops me in my tracks. My mouth goes dry. Of all my brother's friends, he's the most attractive one. And seeing him like this, shirtless and bathed in sunlight, is almost too much to handle.

His body is a masterpiece, his tattoos the brush strokes that define it. Ink traces his neck, his chest, and his abs—a canvas of sharp lines and dark art that makes my mouth water. My eyes drink him in, lingering on the way his muscles shift with each soft breath.

He's a tattooed god.

I've had a crush on him for years, not that he's ever noticed. To him, I'm just his best friend's annoying little sister. Hell, he calls me brat more than my actual name. A word that should make me roll my eyes, but instead, it sends a jolt straight to my core every damn time. It makes me want to get on my knees so he can fix my attitude.

I can't stop staring, my eyes tracing the ridges of his abs, imagining my fingers trailing over them, my tongue following. Heat coils low in my stomach as my gaze dips lower, and my eyes nearly fall out of my head at the sight of the hard outline of his morning wood.

Oh, how I wish I could just sink onto that impressive cock. A rush of heat floods me, my thighs clenching as a wave of heat crashes through me. I try to steady my breathing, but it catches when the deep, gravelly voice that has teased me for years cuts through the silence, and I suppress a moan.

"Take a picture, brat. It'll last longer," Damien muse's, his voice rough with sleep as he drags his forearm off his forehead. His chocolate brown eyes lock on mine, smoldering with a heat that makes my breath hitch. For a brief moment, they dip lower, catching on my hardened nipples. But just as quickly, he looks away.

"In your dreams, playboy," I shoot back with a soft scoff. The nickname is more for me than it is for him—a reminder that he isn't mine and never will be. He has a trail of girls chasing after him. He'd never waste his time on his best friend's bratty baby sister.

I spin on my heel and head for the kitchen, desperate to put some distance between us. "Coffee?" I call over my shoulder.

"Yeah, thanks." His voice is strained, glancing over at him, I see him stretching. I look away before he catches me staring again.

The silence stretches between us while I busy myself with the coffee pot, trying to shake the memory of the heat in his gaze. But when I turn around, two mugs in hand, I freeze. Damien is sitting up now, the book I'd been reading last night in his hands. The book that left me so hot and bothered I had to touch myself on the very spot he's sitting on right now.

A wave of delicious shame crashes over me, my cheeks turning pink as I watch him flip to my bookmark.

"Do you mind?" I snap. Panic rushes through me, and I almost drop his coffee as I race to stop him.

"Not at all," he drawls, smirking up at me as he holds the book just out of reach. It's not exactly unlike him to tease me like this, but my breath still hitches. "My, my," he purrs, closing the book but keeping it in his lap. "I knew you were a brat, but this..." He leans back, letting his eyes sweep over me, heat lingering in their wake. "This explains so much."

"It's just a book, Damien," I snap, my voice sharper than I intend. "It doesn't mean I am actually into that stuff." The words tumble out, half truth, half lie. I don't really know what I'm into. Jake was my first, and he never cared to find out what I liked. The one time I tried to tell him, he looked at me like I'd grown a second head and brushed me off.

Damien doesn't need to know any of that.

But the way he's looking at me now, like he can see just how big of a brat I can be, makes me shift uncomfortably. His smirk widens, and I swear I can see his ego swelling.

He runs a hand through his short, dark brown hair, the strands just long enough for me to imagine tangling my fingers in and grab on. The way his smirk tilts makes me feel he's reading my mind.

"Uh-huh, sure it is," he murmurs, his voice low and teasing.

I clench my jaw, unsure what game he's playing—or even if I'm equipped enough to play along.

Just as I open my mouth to fire back again, Jaxson's sleep-roughened voice cuts through the tension like a bucket of cold water.

"What are you two arguing about now?"

Damien moves away, getting up from the couch just in time for my brother to stroll into the room, his messy blonde hair falling into his eyes and a plain white T-shirt hanging loosely over red boxers.

I roll my eyes, grabbing my coffee and sinking onto the couch, crossing my legs beneath me. "We're not arguing," I mutter, but my tone doesn't carry much conviction.

Damien chuckles, shaking his head smoothly as he reaches the kitchen, leaning over the counter on his elbows, my book still clutched in his hand.

"Why would you think we're arguing?" he asks, voice calm, confident. As if he wasn't just teasing his best friend's baby sister to the point of combustion.

Jaxson raises a brow, clearly unimpressed. "Because you two are always either pushing each other's buttons or arguing. But this early in the morning, I'm betting it's an argument. Ana doesn't function properly until she's had her coffee." He gestures toward my mug, and I lift it in a mock toast, silently acknowledging how well he knows me.

"I was just curious about this book she was reading," Damien says casually, but the mischievous glint in his eye threatens to make my face combust.

Before he can say anything that might embarrass me further, I cut in, my voice a touch too loud. "Have you finished your Christmas shopping?"

Jaxson yawns and stretches, clearly not in a rush. He's as bad at it as I am. "Nope. Still gotta run out today and finish up. You?"

I smile, relieved to steer the conversation somewhere safer. "Just you left. Any chance I can just give you cash?"

He scoffs, rolling his eyes as he grabs a mug from the cabinet. "How about you send me your TBR list, and I'll send you my wishlist?"

"Deal," I say, grinning. It's an easy compromise, and it saves me from spending hours overthinking what he might like.

My attention drifts back to Damien, who's still leaning against the counter. One arm is crossed over his chest, his hand resting in the crook of his elbow as he flips lazily through my book with his other hand. His smirk is maddening, growing wider when he catches me watching him. And then he winks.

Flustered, I drop my gaze and take a sip of my coffee, hoping to hide the warmth creeping into my cheeks.

"Sis, did you check the mail when you got home yesterday?" Jaxson's voice pulls me from my thoughts.

Did I? Right. I did—my new bookish stickers for my Kindle came in. "Yeah, why?" I ask, glancing over at him. He's standing at the kitchen sink, rinsing out his favorite mug.

"The red flag's up," he says, motioning to the mailbox. "And I know you're not the type to send anything that needs a stamp."

I shrug, rolling my eyes at his observation. He knows me too well.

Out of the corner of my eye, I see Damien push off the counter. A moment later, he's next to me on the couch. He doesn't sit too close, but our couch isn't that big, and when he spreads his knees, they brush against mine. The casual touch sends a jolt through me, but I force myself to stay still, refusing to give him the satisfaction of seeing how much he affects me.

"Shit," Jaxson mutters from the kitchen. "I gotta shower. I didn't realize the time—I'm meeting Claire at the coffee shop on campus in thirty."

I laugh in response. He's been trying to hook up with the physics TA ever since he first saw her. As he rushes past, I call after him, "When are you going to give it up? You're not her type."

He stops just long enough to shoot back, "Then why did she agree to meet me after the semester ended?"

Damn. He's got a point.

Damien's knee nudges mine, and his deep voice rumbles, "He's not wrong."

I shrug, not willing to admit defeat. The silence that follows after Jaxson leaves is thick, charged, the kind that demands to be broken. But I bite my tongue, unwilling to be the one to do it.

After what feels like an eternity, I grab my phone, opening Spotify to play my favorite playlist.

"Use Jax's account," Damien says. It's not a question.

Living up to my nickname, I smirk. "Nope."

His answering grin tells me he was expecting that. Before I can react, he leans over and tries to grab the remote from my hand.

"Uh, I don't think so," I say, moving to tuck it under my thigh.

Unfazed, Damien takes my coffee mug and places it on the table. His eyes gleam with mischief, and I realize too late that I've walked straight into his trap.

"Don't you dare," I warn, scooting back against the couch.

He doesn't say anything, just smirks and pounces, his fingers finding my sides and tickling me mercilessly.

"Damien!" I shriek, squirming under his touch as laughter bubbles out of me.

"Brat," he growls, leaning closer. "Give. Me. The. Remote."

I shake my head, laughing harder, my grip on the remote faltering. Desperate, I roll onto my back and shove it behind me, keeping it pinned beneath me. His hands don't stop, though, tickling me until I can barely breathe.

Then, suddenly, he stops.

His weight shifts, and I freeze when I realize the position we're in. He's kneeling between my legs, his body hovering over mine. His pelvis is so close that I swear I can feel the heat of him through our clothes.

His gaze drops to where my shirt has ridden up, exposing a strip of bare skin just above my waistband. My breath catches. Neither of us moves.

When his eyes meet mine, they darken—no, his pupils dilate. The shift in his expression sends a jolt through me, and before I can react, his gaze drops to the strip of exposed skin above my waistband.

His thumb brushes over it, his touch so light it makes me shiver. I whimper, the sound escaping before I can stop it. My body betrays me further when my hips shift, rocking against him, and I feel his cock—hard, hot, and pressing against me.

He leans down, his lips brushing my ear, his voice a low growl. "Is this what you want, brat? To be treated like the girls in those books?"

The words send heat pooling between my thighs, and then his hands are on me—one fisting the fabric of my shirt, the other tangling in my hair, tugging my head back so I have no choice but to meet his gaze. His dark eyes burn into mine as he rolls his hips, the friction of his hard length against my dampening pussy drawing a moan of his name from my lips.

That's all the confirmation he needs.

He chuckles darkly, the sound sending a shiver down my spine, and his tongue darts out to trace the shell of my ear. The sensation snaps me out of my haze.

I push against his chest, my breath ragged. "Here. Take the remote, asshole." I shove it into his hand and scramble out from under him. "I'm going to check the mail and get ready."

For a second, he doesn't move. His expression flickers with something I can't quite place—confusion, hesitation, regret—but then he shifts back, giving me space. I hurry off the couch, needing distance, needing to breathe.

His voice stops me just as I reach the door.

"I'm sorry, Anastasia." He sounds strained, like he's forcing the words out. "I don't know what came over me."

The apology feels like a slap. I don't look back as I step outside, letting the cool air hit my overheated skin. It doesn't just cool me down; it numbs the ache spreading through my chest.

Because I know what he didn't say. It won't happen again.

I hug myself against the chill, thankful I'd had the sense to put on my slippers. The mailbox isn't far, just a few steps down and a short walk across the driveway. The brisk air helps, though not enough to fully extinguish the lingering heat or dull the sting of his rejection.

But when I open the mailbox, the air around me seems to freeze.

Inside is a neatly folded maroon t-shirt, the fabric stained with something white and dried. A note sits on top, the handwriting elegant but unfamiliar. My hands tremble as I pick it up and read the words:

'On the first night of Christmas, I gift my angel the seed I spent thinking of fucking her until she knows no man but me.'

Him

My little angel is the girl of my dreams. I've known that for a while now. The moment I realized she was the one was when I saw her curled up with one of those dirty books she loves so much. She was so engrossed, her fingers gripping the pages, her thighs clenching just a little. I could barely breathe. I had to know what had her so worked up.

I tracked down the book, and as I read through it, I was shocked—but intrigued. It was about a masked man obsessed with a girl. She had no idea he was watching her, planning to make her his. Little does my angel know, I'm already that man. And her fantasy is about to become her reality.

Since then, I've kept tabs on the books she devours, her secret little worlds of submission and desire. Each one gives me another piece of the puzzle, another hint at what she craves in the dark corners of her mind. I want her to live out every sinful dream she's ever had—because she's mine. But nothing could have prepared me for what I've learned about her.

My sweet, innocent angel has the soul of a filthy little slut.

I wasn't there to see her reaction to the gift I left last night, but watching her now, it's clear she enjoyed it. She's standing in the kitchen, making a late-night snack, her hair slightly messy, her body bathed in the soft glow of the stove light. But that's not what has my dick aching.

It's the shirt.

My shirt.

The one I left for her, soaked with my cum. She's wearing it. And as if that weren't enough, she lifts the collar to her nose and inhales, her lashes fluttering as though she can smell me.

Fuck.

She knows I'm watching her. She has to. She chose to wear the shirt covered in my cum.

I pull out my phone, knowing I'll want to remember what she does next.

She climbs onto the kitchen island, facing the window, the same window I'm standing outside of, hidden by the dark. If it were daylight, she'd see me. I can't keep my eyes off her, and I'm almost certain she can feel my gaze, the way it devours her, because she starts to put on a show.

She wants me to see what she's doing.

She leans back, dragging her hands over the fabric that barely covers her, her fingers tracing the curve of her tits before sliding down her stomach. When she reaches the hem, she spreads her legs wide, and my breath catches in my throat.

No panties.

She's bare, glistening, the proof of her arousal visible even from here.

My angel starts to rub slow, lazy circles over her clit, teasing herself as if she has all the time in the world. Her lips part, and I swear I can almost hear her soft moans through the glass. She's so fucking wet, her fingers sliding easily against her slick folds. Then she does something that almost breaks me.

She brings her fingers to her lips, tasting herself.

I grip my phone, my hands shaking. There's no way I'm not recording this. She works herself faster, her hips bucking as her pleasure builds. Within minutes, her thighs clench, and her entire body trembles. She rides out her orgasm beautifully, and I have to stifle a groan of my own.

But it's what she does next that sends me over the edge.

With shaking hands, she drags her wet fingers over my shirt—the same shirt stained with my cum—smearing her release into the marks I left behind. She's combining us, claiming me the way I've already claimed her.

Fuck.

My cock is painfully hard, but I don't have time to deal with that right now. Her brother will be back in a few hours, and I need to move fast.

I know exactly what her gift for tonight will be.

But first, I have work to do.

Her

I wake up feeling invigorated, the memory of last night coursing through me like a live wire. Whoever left me that filthy gift yesterday was watching me. I could feel his eyes on me, heavy and unrelenting. I don't know who he is, but I know he made me feel things I shouldn't—not for a man who should terrify me.

I crossed a line last night. Letting him watch me wasn't just indulgent; it was deliberate. I couldn't help it, I wanted him to see me. Craved it. And now, just thinking about it sends pinpricks of pleasure skittering through my veins.

How could it not? It feels like I'm living out the plot of one of my own books. My thoughts spiral, trying to piece together who this man might be, even as I wash my face, slip on a pair of shorts, and head to the kitchen in search of coffee.

The rich scent of fresh brew hits me before I round the corner, and my pace quickens. But when I step into the kitchen, the sight that greets me stops me in my tracks.

A shirtless, tattooed back.

The kind of back I'd love to rake my nails across.

Damien.

He turns, catching me staring—again. But today, something's shifted. The air between us crackles with tension, thick and electric. His dark eyes drop to my bare thighs, then leisurely drag up my body. They linger—just long enough to make my pulse race—before meeting mine.

He chuckles, low and rich, and says, "You know, I'd say you need to get laid, but it looks like you already have."

His chin tilts toward me, and I glance down, mortified. The shirt. I slept in *his* shirt.

Shit.

"It's not—I didn't—" I stammer, scrambling for an explanation, but my words fizzle out when he starts toward me.

Closing the space between us.

Invading it.

His breath brushes my ear as he leans in, voice a husky whisper. "It's kinda hot, seeing you like this."

The hem of the shirt I'm wearing is between his fingers now, toying, teasing.

I must have misheard him. I must have. But the hard bulge pressing against my stomach says otherwise.

Instinctively, my palms find his chest, and I regret it almost instantly. The feel of his skin under my hands—the heat, the strength—makes me want to pull him closer, not push him away.

But I find the willpower. Somehow.

Damien steps back, his lips quirking into a knowing smirk.

"Don't fuck with me, Damien," I snap, forcing steel into my voice. "I'm not in the mood. Besides, I don't even know who it is anyway."

Shit. I didn't mean to say that.

But he and my brother mess around enough that, with any luck, he'll assume I'm just talking about some random hookup. At least, I hope so.

He raises an eyebrow at me, his smirk both infuriating and irresistible. "Oh, so the little brat finally got laid. Does that mean you'll start playing nice?"

I roll my eyes, but my stomach twists. I hate that he calls me that—hate it because it makes my pulse race every time. "No, I didn't get laid," I snap, maybe a little too quickly.

He tilts his head, dark eyes narrowing as he studies me, trying to piece it together. Too late, I realize my mistake. I scramble to recover, forcing a sharp smile. "I'll still be your best friend's bratty little sister. You know, the one you so *clearly* love tormenting."

I push past him, ignoring how close he is, and reach for a mug from the cupboard above the coffee pot. My hand shakes just slightly, but I don't think he notices—or at least, I hope he doesn't.

"Clearly she's all grown up," he mutters, voice thick with mockery. "Covered in cum."

I freeze.

"Maybe next time, it could be mine."

The last part is so quiet, so low, I almost convince myself I misheard him. But the image that slams into my mind tells me I didn't.

I see myself on my knees in front of him, his hand tangled in my hair, holding me in place as he groans, shooting ropes of his release across my face. The thought shifts, hot and unrelenting—Damien straddling me, his powerful thighs framing mine, stroking himself with rough, urgent motions until he marks me. His cum dripping onto this shirt, staking his claim.

Heat flares across my skin, and I shake my head, desperate to banish the images before they consume me. My throat is dry, and I clear it, ready to ask what he meant. Ready to call him out.

But I don't get the chance.

My brother stumbles into the kitchen, groaning like death warmed over, clearly hungover. He doesn't look at either of us as he pours a cup of coffee, grabs the aspirin bottle, and yanks a water from the fridge. "Morning," he grunts, before shuffling off back downstairs.

I exhale slowly, willing the tension in the room to ease.

Damien leaves me in the kitchen, grabbing his shirt on his way out. He pauses at the door, glancing back. "I'm going to get him some food. Want anything?"

I shake my head. "No, I've got plans this morning."

He nods and steps outside. I linger at the window, watching as he crosses the yard. When he reaches the mailbox, he turns, disappearing around the corner. My eyes flick to the little red flag, raised and waiting.

Something churns in my chest—excitement, anticipation, maybe even dread. I rush to the living room, slipping into my shoes, and head out to check the mail. My pulse quickens with every step, my curiosity a live wire.

When I open the mailbox, I freeze.

Inside is a small brown box, wrapped with a crimson bow. I can't help but smile at the careful detail, the deliberate effort. But when I'm back in my room, door locked, and I open the box, the contents make my breath hitch.

Inside are several pictures.

Of me.

From last night.

I'm sprawled on the counter, lost in the haze of pleasure, touching myself in his cum-soaked t-shirt, the fabric clinging to my skin.

Nestled among the pictures is a note:

'The things I will do to you, my little angel. Seeing you covered in my cum, mixing yours with mine, gave me ideas—ones I will surely make happen.'

Heat pools low in my belly as I reread the words, my hands trembling.

I thought I'd satisfied that itch last night. I thought I'd taken the edge off, scratched the surface of whatever this is. But this man—this mystery—ignites something deeper in me, something dark and thrilling. It's insane, I know that. Borderline psychotic. I should tell someone.

But I haven't thought about Jake since yesterday morning, and haven't felt the ache of loss. Instead, there's this. A distraction. A dangerous, electric distraction that consumes me.

And then there's Damien.

Things between us have shifted—there's no denying that. He's hell-bent on working me up, pushing buttons I didn't know I had. The tension crackles between us, charged and undeniable. But he's my brother's best friend. He's off-limits, and I know it.

Still, my thoughts drift back to the pictures in my hand. Maybe something could happen with my mystery man. My thighs press together involuntarily, heat building fast. If I don't take care of this now, today is going to be unbearable.

I cross to my bedside table, opening the drawer to retrieve my blue rabbit vibrator. This one usually keeps the edge off for a few days.

Hopefully, it will be enough now.

I slip out of my shorts, leaving the shirt on, the fabric still heavy with his scent. Turning on my toy, I feel the hum beneath my fingers. It has two settings: one for thrusting and another for the clit attachment to vibrate. Both have always been reliable, but today feels different.

I crawl into bed, the anticipation building as I lay back and part my thighs. Holding the toy at my center, I rub its head against my clit, teasing myself. The sensation makes my body jolt, a rush of heat flooding through me. Slowly, I trail it down to my entrance, sliding it in just a little before pulling it out again. In, out—each time deeper—until it's fully seated inside me. The rabbit ears rest perfectly against my clit, sending tiny pulses of pleasure through me even before I turn the vibration on.

I take a shaky breath, leaving it still for a moment, before flipping the thruster on. A groan escapes my lips as the sensation takes over, and I arch into the feeling. With my free hand, I pinch my nipple through the fabric of the shirt, the friction sparking a deeper ache inside me.

I start moving the toy, slowly at first, pushing it deeper, pulling it out, fucking myself harder. My hips rise to meet it as I turn up the vibration, chasing that edge, trying to lose myself in the pleasure. But my focus falters.

My hand drifts lower, sliding beneath the hem of the shirt to cup my bare breast. My fingers graze the faint stains on the fabric, and the memory of Damien's words comes rushing back: *"Maybe next time, it could be mine."*

A vision of him flashes in my mind—him standing over me, watching me, his hand stroking himself as he claims my body, his cum painting my skin, dripping between my thighs. The thought hits me like a tidal wave, and my legs snap shut, locking the toy deep inside me as the first orgasm crashes over me. I scream his name, my body shaking uncontrollably, my breath catching in my throat.

But the toy doesn't stop. It keeps working, relentless, driving me higher even as I struggle to come down. Another vision floods my mind: Damien spreading my legs wide, his hands gripping me tight, his dick sinking into me, stretching me as I lay bound beneath him, nothing more than a toy for him to use.

The second orgasm tears through me, just as intense as the first. My body trembles, teetering on the edge of overstimulation. My slit aches from the unrelenting pressure, but I can't bring myself to stop. The thought of Damien—his weight pinning me down, his cock pounding into me, his low groans filling the room—drives me over the edge once more. A smaller, softer wave washes through me, quenching the heat that's burned inside me for weeks.

Finally, I manage to turn the toy off and pull it out, my body still trembling. My breathing is ragged as I lay there, limbs heavy with exhaustion and satisfaction.

Then, an idea strikes me—a bold, reckless, crazy idea.

I clean the toy off on the shirt, his stains and mine mingling together. I pull the shirt off and use it to wipe the slick mess between my thighs. Once I've calmed down, I get up, take a long, hot shower, and get dressed for the day.

As I head out, I make a mental note: stop by the store later for a box, wrapping paper, and a bow.

Him

I've been counting down the hours until I could see my little angel again. All day, my thoughts have been consumed by her—how she looked last night, the way she touched herself in that shirt, knowing I was watching. As I make my way down her street, I can't help but wonder if she'll wear it again, or put on another show just for me. One of these days, I'll tell her how proud I am of her, and praise her for being such a good girl for me.

I don't know why I chose to go about everything this way. Maybe it was the look on her face when she found my brother balls-deep in their tutor—the pain in her eyes when she realized the person she was supposed to be with betrayed her. I knew that she needed a distraction, something thrilling, something *fun*, before diving into another relationship.

I've had a thing for her for years, even before Jake. I could never bring myself to say anything, though, and when she started dating him, I told myself it would pass. I'd grow over it. But I didn't. My infatuation turned into something deeper, something undeniable. And I know she's hurt, hesitant to let someone get close again.

But I've waited long enough. And now, she'll be mine.

When I reach my spot under the tree, hidden by shadows and my black hoodie, I watch her. She seems lighter today, like a weight has been lifted, her steps quicker, her movements more carefree. It's Monday—movie night with her brother. Usually, they invite friends, so I know my time here is limited. If people show up, I'll have to leave early. I can't risk being caught, or I'll have some explaining to do.

Still, I needed to see her tonight. I brought another gift for her. This little gift has become something I look forward to, each night building her curiosity. Like *The Twelve Days Of Christmas*, but my gifts are far from innocent. I'll tease her, tempt her, until Christmas Eve—when I will finally reveal myself. By then, she'll be begging for me.

But not before I've had my fun.

Slipping toward the mailbox to leave tonight's gift, I notice something strange—the red flag is up. My curiosity spikes. What could possibly be left there?

When I open it, I freeze.

There's a small box inside, wrapped in white paper, a red ribbon and bow tied neatly on top. A note sits on it, addressed to me:

'To my mystery man.'

My pulse quickens. Without hesitation, I take the box and stuff the paper and ribbon into my hoodie pocket, hiding any trace of it. I tear the lid off, and look inside.

My cock hardens instantly.

My little angel has given me my shirt back. But it's not just my shirt—it's covered in new stains. Stains *she* made.

A low groan escapes my lips as I take in the sight of it, the fabric still faintly damp in places. She's such a filthy, perfect little brat, teasing me like this. I almost miss the folded note tucked inside, but when I pick it up, the faint floral scent of her perfume hits me. She sprayed it just for me.

Ducking deeper behind the tree, I use the glow from my phone screen to read:

'It felt appropriate to give you your shirt back. I hope you don't mind—I needed to clean myself up after I fucked myself with a toy this morning after I received your gift. Enjoy.'

She ended it with a winky face and a heart.

My little angel will be the death of me.

I grip the box tightly, my mind racing. I might have to rethink tonight's gift—this game has escalated faster than I anticipated. But then I glance at the shirt again, my fingers brushing the stained fabric, and an idea strikes me.

Oh, I know exactly what to give her.

Her

Last night was our weekly movie night. It used to be just Jaxson and me, but over the past few years, Damien and Amara have become staples of the tradition. Last night was no exception. Now, Amara's currently passed out in my bed while I go fetch us some coffee. Feeling cooped up, I decide to get out of the house and walk to the café down the block—they make my favorite drink, and their bagels are amazing, too.

As I try to sneak out quietly, Damien catches me in the kitchen. Of course, he has to make some comment, the kind only he can deliver, designed to needle me just enough to linger. That man has a talent for getting under my skin. I leave in a huff, his laughter trailing after me as I shut the door. On the walk to the café, I mumble all the clever comebacks I should have said, working myself up for no reason. I even laugh out loud at one point—because, let's be honest, he'd probably have some infuriating retort to that, too.

I don't understand what's happening between us. First, there was that moment on the couch the other morning. Then his comment yesterday. And now today. It feels like he's deliberately toeing a line, pushing me into territory I don't know how to navigate. His words strip me down in ways I can't process.

And the truth? I wouldn't mind his hands on me, his lips on mine—or more. I wouldn't mind his dick in any of my holes, his cum claiming every part of me, leaving me breathless and marked in ways I'd never forget. But it's more than that. It's the fact that his words get to me, dig beneath the surface in a way no one else's ever have. But nothing can happen between us. Not ever. And we both know it.

Still, lately, he's been acting like he doesn't care about those unspoken rules. And that terrifies me. Because if I let myself believe he wants me—for more than a fleeting moment, for more than just a game—I know he'd deny me. And he has his reasons. Good ones. Reasons I can't argue with, no matter how much I might want to.

I sigh heavily as I open the door to the coffee shop. The scent of roasting beans, the low hum of conversation, and baristas shouting names all hit me at once. I take a deep breath. The familiar atmosphere here is a balm to my frayed nerves, a brief reprieve from the chaos Damien seems to stir in me without even trying.

I stifle a laugh, though uneasiness curls in my gut. It should stem from the stalker I have—*should* being the keyword—but no, today just feels…off. That's why I came here for coffee. I needed this place. The morning hustle of people going through their routines helps me do the same. Grounding me.

After placing my order, I step to the side, letting myself blend into the background as I watch the crowd move. My mind drifts, chasing thoughts I can't seem to pin down.

I'm snapped back when my name is called. Shaking off the daze, I weave through the throng of bodies, grab my drink, and thank the barista before heading home. But that uneasy feeling clings to me, like an itch I can't quite scratch. The sensation of being watched prickles the back of my neck. Usually, that feeling carries a strange comfort—a familiarity—but not today. Today, it feels invasive, unsettling.

My steps quicken, heart pounding harder with each one. I've always been grateful for living so close to campus, but never more than I am in this moment.

The unease doesn't fade until I'm inside, the door firmly shut behind me. Only then do I take my first full breath. Forcing myself to move quietly, I head toward my room. But the quiet house reassures me—the couch is empty.

When I open my door, Amara is sprawled on my bed, scrolling on her phone.

"I should have guessed," I say, lifting an eyebrow.

She spots the coffee in my hand and perks up. Sitting up, she reaches for her iced peppermint mocha. "Just what I needed this morning," she says, taking the cup with a grateful smile.

I wrap my hands around my peppermint hot chocolate, letting the warmth seep into my skin. Taking a sip, I feel the heat melt some of my tension, like a balm for my rattled nerves.

"I told you and Jaxson that drinking game was a bad idea," I say, leaning against the doorframe.

Amara rolls her eyes. She and my brother had started some ridiculous game last night—completely unrelated to the movie. The rules? Any time one of us looked at our phones, it was a shot. It got out of hand fast. At one point, Amara was texting Jaxson under the table, just to make his phone go off. She'd pulled his name up at the cost of a shot and then sent him random nonsense. It worked, too. She got him to look three times before he blocked her for the night.

"Yeah, yeah," she says, brushing me off with a grin. "We had a blast, and you know it."

She's not wrong.

"I'm going to take a shower before I head out," she says, gathering her things.

I raise a questioning eyebrow.

"No, I'm not seeing anyone," she clarifies, rolling her eyes again. "I just need to pick up my new jacket for the trip this weekend. I scheduled a pickup. I'm not dealing with last-minute shoppers."

I shrug in agreement, watching as she disappears into the bathroom.

We keep a few things at each other's places since we're always crashing at one another's homes. With nothing planned for the rest of the day except reading, I strip out of my clothes, pull on my favorite plush robe, and crawl back into bed.

While Amara is occupied, I grab my phone and start clearing notifications.

That's when I see it—a message from an unknown number.

I don't think twice before clicking on it, my thumb hovering over the screen. The preview shows...images. Familiar ones. My stomach drops as realization sinks in. The message contains a video.

The audio, faint but unmistakable, sends heat rushing to my face. My pulse quickens as I close the message with trembling hands.

Not now. Not with Amara here.

If she sees this, or senses something's wrong, she'll push. And if she pushes, I'll break. I'm not ready for anyone to know—not yet.

Swallowing hard, I set the phone down and force myself to breathe. Whatever this is, it can wait. For now.

To distract myself, I retreat to my library, seeking solace among my books. But the moment I step inside, my plans for escape shatter. Damien is sitting in one of my oversized chairs, deeply engrossed in one of my books.

Of course, he doesn't have a shirt on. That doesn't shock me anymore. But I'll never get used to the sight of his bare, tattooed chest.

My eyes betray me, drinking him in. His hair is damp from a recent shower, stray droplets clinging to his skin, tracing paths over the intricate ink covering his chest. His gaze is locked on the pages in front of him, like the words are answers to questions he's spent a lifetime asking.

But then I recognize the book he's reading. It's one of my spicy ones.

I'm not ashamed of my reading preferences, but something about the way his brows furrow as he reads makes my stomach flip. It's like he's studying the text with an intensity that feels...dangerous.

I clear my throat, trying to draw his attention. He doesn't immediately look up. Instead, he takes his time, finishing whatever passage he's on before finally acknowledging me.

His head stays tilted toward the book, but his eyes slowly lift to meet mine.

I forget how to breathe.

His gaze is molten, a slow-burning heat that travels down my body like wildfire. My robe suddenly feels insubstantial under the weight of his stare.

When his hands move, my attention shifts to them. One rests lazily on the arm of the chair, while the other keeps the book open, fingers splayed across the pages. He notices my focus, and his lips curl into a knowing smirk. Without breaking eye contact, his fingers begin to stroke the middle of the book, dragging down the crease with deliberate precision.

All I can think about is what it would feel like for him to touch *me* like that, to spread me open with the same care.

My thighs clench involuntarily, seeking relief I refuse to give myself. His smirk deepens, as if he knows exactly what's running through my mind.

"You know," he says, his voice low and teasing, "I figured out the other morning that you read dirty books. But tell me—do you get off by them too?"

Heat rushes to my cheeks, and I stomp forward, reaching for the book, desperate to steer this conversation away from dangerous waters. "What I read—and what I do or don't do while reading—is none of your business," I huff, snatching it from his hand.

But the moment I grab the book, he stands abruptly, bringing us nose-to-nose.

"Tsk, tsk, tsk," he clicks his tongue, each sound slow and deliberate.

I instinctively back up with every step he takes forward, the distance between us shrinking until my back hits the bookshelf. My heart races as I realize there's nowhere else to go.

He lifts one arm, planting it beside my head, caging me in. His other hand reclaims the book, effortlessly flipping it open to the page he'd been reading. He holds it there, his fingers still splayed across the spine, while his eyes burn into mine.

"I wasn't finished," he murmurs, and then—like it's the most natural thing in the world—he starts reading aloud.

His deep voice sends shivers down my spine as he reads, *"Did you go in there to get yourself off?" Before she can respond, I press her against the wall, caging her in, shutting out the rest of the world. "And what if I did?" she fires back, though her voice wavers under the intensity of my stare.*

Damien leans closer, his hardening length pressing into me. "Oh, look. She's a brat just like you," he murmurs, his words laced with amusement and something darker.

"I am not a brat," I say, though the breathless tone betrays me. His smirk deepens once more, making my pulse race. Okay, maybe I am a brat, but only for him.

His eyes flicker to my lips before darting back to the book in his hand. He doesn't stop there, continuing to read aloud in that low, sinful voice. *"Since you won't tell me, I guess I'll just have to check myself. Open up, sweet girl."* He pauses and taps my thigh, imitating the action described in the story.

I freeze, unsure of what he wants. The hesitation only seems to amuse him further. He leans down, grips the back of my thigh, and lifts it to rest on his hip.

The split in my robe shifts, exposing more of my leg. His gaze locks with mine, and I swear I see a storm raging in his brown eyes, pulling me under. My heart skips a beat, hammering wildly in my chest.

His fingers trail up my ankle, brushing my calf before reaching my thigh. Every touch sends heat coursing through me. By the time his hand grazes my hip, I gasp, rolling my hips against his hardness without thinking. His sharp intake of breath is matched by a deep, guttural groan when he realizes I'm not wearing panties.

"You were made to torment me," he growls, his grip tightening on my hip, firm enough to bruise.

The book slips from his hand, forgotten as he grips my other side, holding me steady. His thumb brushes the underside of my breast, sending a fresh wave of heat through my body, and an involuntary whimper leaves my throat. I need more—I need *him*. "You aren't wearing anything under this, are you?"

All I can do is shake my head.

My silence drives him further. His hips grind into me, his arousal undeniable, the friction dizzying. I feel myself unraveling, the tension coiling tighter and tighter.

But before anything can progress, I hear my name being called from my bedroom.

Damien freezes. His jaw tightens as he releases me and steps back, adjusting himself as if nothing had happened. My breath comes in shallow gasps, and without a word, I slip out of the library to see why Amara interrupted us.

Once I'm in the safety of my room, with walls and doors between us, I realize my entire body is trembling with need. My skin feels too tight, my mind racing with what could've happened if Amara hadn't called my name.

"Ana," she says from the bed, her voice laced with concern, "what's going on? Did something happen? You look like you did that time you walked in on Damien and that blonde."

I shake my head quickly, trying to dispel the thought, but I know I'm not okay. I feel torn, pulled in two different directions, and I have no idea how to handle it.

"I have no clue what just happened," I admit, sinking onto the bed beside her. She sits quietly as I spill everything—the tension, the moments between Damien and me over the past few days. I don't hold back, letting it all pour out.

"It's not like anything could ever happen between us anyway," I finish, my voice soft. "Even if I did sleep with him, it wouldn't be more than that. I can't do that—I can't be just another fling. I want all or nothing with him."

The confession weighs heavily on me, but it's not the whole truth. My thoughts stray to my mystery man, the one who makes me feel like my darkest desires are not only okay but welcomed. With him, I feel like I'd be safe to act out everything I've kept buried.

But I keep his existence to myself—for now.

Amara pulls me into a hug, her arms warm and comforting. "I understand. I just want you to be happy, Ana," she whispers, squeezing me tighter.

"I know," I say, my response muffled against her shoulder.

The problem is, I don't know what—or who—will make me happy. The mystery man who seems to hold all my hidden desires, or the one man I'm certain I can never truly have.

Her

Amara spends most of the day finding excuses to stay with me. I don't blame her—after everything I told her earlier, I can see the concern etched on her face. But halfway through the first movie, I suddenly remember that I forgot to check the mail this morning.

"Isn't it time to go pick up your jacket?" I say, as I pause the movie. Then follow her out the door to ensure she leaves.

Amara shifts in the doorway, clearly debating whether to argue, but I cut her off with a reassuring smile. "I'm fine. Go grab your jacket; you've been talking about it all day. I'll be here when you get back."

She hesitates for a moment longer before sighing. "Okay. But I'm coming back tonight for a girl's night—no arguments."

"Deal," I reply, practically pushing her out the door.

Once she's gone, I head to the mailbox, half-expecting to find something waiting for me. But when I open it, I'm greeted by nothing but emptiness.

The wave of disappointment that washes over me takes me by surprise. I hadn't realized how much I'd already come to anticipate gifts from my mystery man. They'd become a strange constant, a thrill that, despite the circumstances, I couldn't ignore.

I linger at the mailbox for a moment longer before heading back inside. That's when it hits me—I never checked the message from the unknown number earlier.

Rushing upstairs to the sanctuary of my room, I grab my phone and open the message.

It doesn't take long for my heart to start racing.

The text reads:

> One day soon, it won't be the pictures; it will be you.

Attached is a video.

My finger hovers over the play button for the briefest of moments before curiosity overtakes me. I press it.

The video begins with pictures. Pictures of me.

I'm perched on the edge of a kitchen island, my legs crossed casually, but the sight makes my stomach drop. It's not my kitchen—the sleek gray-and-marble countertops are nothing like mine.

I stare at the screen, trying to make sense of what I'm seeing. The images aren't just candid—they're intimate, as though captured during a moment I should have been alone.

My pulse quickens, a mix of fear and something else crawling up my spine.

Heavy breathing assaults my ears, followed by a deep, guttural groan from a man. The sound sends a jolt straight through me, my insides clenching around nothing. My thighs press together instinctively, seeking friction that isn't there.

"Fuck, little angel, squeeze this cock," the voice moans, low and rough, dripping with need.

The realization hits me like a punch: he's pleasuring himself to the thought of me. Not just anyone, but *me*. He's imagining I'm the one he's buried in—not his fist. The thought sends a wave of heat through my body, and before I know it, my hand slips inside my shorts, fingers seeking the ache between my thighs.

His breaths grow heavier, his moans more urgent, and the sound of his strokes becomes faster, more desperate. His rhythm, the way he's unraveling for me, pushes me closer to the edge than I thought possible.

"Fuck, Ana," he curses, his voice thick and guttural, followed by the sound of his release.

The thought of him spilling hot ropes of cum while thinking about me, while saying my name, sends me over the edge. My release crashes through me, sharp and all-consuming. But when the high fades, I realize it's not enough. Not lately. Between him and Damien, it's *never* enough.

Groaning in frustration, I replay the video, focusing on the sounds he makes. There's something intoxicating about knowing I've driven him to this point, made him desperate for release. His groans, his growls, his ragged breaths—all because of me. It awakens something deep and possessive inside, a part of me that craves this power, this control. The idea of making someone so undone that they can't hold back—that they want me so badly they can't help but show it—satisfies something primal in me.

I watch the video a few more times before admitting to myself that I need to stop. My body's trembling, my thoughts scattered, and the tension in my chest refuses to fade.

A shower. That's what I need—a long, scalding shower to clear my head.

Stripping off my clothes, I step into the steaming water, letting it cascade over me. I take a seat on the small bench in the corner, resting my elbows on my knees and burying my face in my hands.

The water's heat seeps into my tense muscles, easing the knots in my shoulders, but my thoughts remain relentless.

I think about Damien and the last few days—his teasing, the way he gets under my skin, the way he looks at me like I'm something he's ready to devour.

I think about my mystery man, the way he's unlocked something inside me I didn't even realize was there. The intensity of it, the thrill of it, both terrify and excite me.

And then I think about my brother. How would he react if he knew what had been happening with his best friend?

Who am I kidding? I know exactly how it would go.

Back when I was a freshman in highschool, my brother's best friend at the time was Seth. The quintessential boy-next-door with short blonde hair and striking green eyes, Seth was every girl's dream—and that year, he wanted me. He made me feel special, told me how much I meant to him, and when he kissed me, I thought I was floating.

But when Jax found out, everything came crashing down.

He went full big-brother mode, telling Seth in no uncertain terms that none of his friends were good enough for his baby sister, especially him. Their friendship fell apart, and a few months later, Jax met Damien. I remember how clear he made it to Damien from the beginning: *Anastasia is off-limits. Always.*

And Damien respected that—for years.

Until recently.

Thinking about Seth and how devastated Jax was when he found out about us, I know I can't do this. I can't let myself pursue Damien, no matter how much I want to. I have to accept it, as painful as it is. If I don't, it won't just hurt Jax—it'll destroy me, too.

I'll have to start building walls around myself again, thick enough to keep Damien out. And as for my mystery man? He's nothing more than a distraction, but I'll take it. Anything to help keep my focus off Damien.

When my thoughts start drifting to Jake—the mistake I refuse to let myself revisit—I know it's time to shake this off. With a sigh, I turn off the shower, grab a towel, and dry off before stepping into my bedroom.

I'm not surprised to find Amara sprawled across my bed, phone in hand, texting away.

"Did you get your jacket?" I ask, digging through my drawer to find a black pair of panties.

Without looking up, she hums, "I did. Also got you a matching one, because I'm extra like that."

I roll my eyes with a chuckle. "Of course you did."

Sliding on a shirt and leggings—deciding to skip the bra—I walk to my closet and pull out two boxes, placing them in plain view. Amara doesn't glance up until I speak.

"Which is why *I* got these."

That gets her attention. Her eyes snap up to see me holding two boxes of new Uggs.

She laughs, a bright, carefree sound. "You got us matching shoes?"

"Of course! We've got to look our best, especially this weekend."

Amara sits up, shaking her head with a grin. "Matching jackets and shoes—this is why we work so well."

I smirk, returning the boots to the closet and glancing at my partially packed duffle bag. "Have you figured out what you're wearing Saturday night for the Christmas party?"

She scoffs, throwing her phone down. "When have you ever known me to plan ahead like that?"

"Fair enough," I say with a laugh, "but you can always borrow something of mine if you want."

"Tempting," she replies, her grin widening.

Amara hops up, heading straight for the closet. Halfway there, she stops in her tracks and spins back around to face me.

"Wait, what are you wearing? I don't want to accidentally pick your dress as an option."

I grin, heading into my walk-in closet and pulling out the dress I'd already picked. It's a fitted, emerald green long-sleeve dress with a square neckline. The back scoops low, nearly grazing my lower back, and a thigh-high slit adds the perfect finishing touch.

Amara's eyes widen, and her mouth drops open. "That is stunning! You're going to look incredible in it." Then her eyes light up mischievously. "So... does that mean the burgundy dress with the tulle skirt is up for grabs?"

I laugh, knowing she'd ask for it. She'd mentioned it months ago when we first started planning to go to the party. "Yep," I say with a nod. "Fresh from the cleaners. I picked it up yesterday."

She squeals in excitement, immediately grabbing the dress and laying it across the bed before starting to strip down. I laugh and follow suit, pulling off my clothes. It's an unspoken ritual between us: we always face away from each other while changing, just for the dramatic reveal.

As I adjust my dress, Amara calls out, "Ready?"

I count down. "Three... two... one."

We turn to face each other, and I can't stop the grin from spreading across my face. "That dress was made for you," I tell her honestly.

Though the burgundy dress had been meant for me, it fits Amara like a dream. The gown hugs her hips and narrow waist perfectly, the fabric accentuating her figure. The back laces down to her waistline, giving it a romantic edge, while the deep V-neck plunges just past her breasts. But the real showstopper is the sheer tulle overlay that flares out at the waist like a modern train—not long enough to drag behind but still dramatic enough to make a statement.

Her fair complexion glows against the rich burgundy color, and her chestnut brown hair, flowing in loose waves, completes the look.

She giggles, twirling a little. "Babe, no man could deny you in that dress."

I smirk, adjusting my own emerald gown. "Speak for yourself—you're going to have a line of admirers waiting for you all night."

We share a knowing look, already on the same page.

"JAXSON! DAMIEN!" We yell in unison, just as I pull my hair out of the messy bun, letting it cascade in waves over my shoulders. The guys open the door just in time.

"What are you two yelling about now?" Jax asks, his voice tinged with amusement, with Damien stepping in right behind him. But the moment they both cross the threshold, they freeze.

Jaxson's eyes sweep over Amara, his interest obvious. But it's Damien's gaze that holds me captive. The intensity of it burns through me, making my nipples tighten in response.

"Fuck me," Damien murmurs under his breath, his voice so low I almost didn't catch it.

Jax clears his throat, snapping me back to reality. "You two look amazing," he says, though his gaze never strays from Amara. It's as if the world outside of her doesn't exist.

Amara brushes a stray strand of hair behind her ear, slightly flustered. "Umm, thank you," she replies, a faint blush creeping across her cheeks.

When they finally leave, we both exhale in relief, a nervous laugh bubbling from us.

"What was that?" I ask, still processing the tension that filled the room.

"I have no idea," she breathes, still wide-eyed. "I don't think he's ever looked at me like that."

I know about Amara's past crush on Jax before she and her ex got together, and I always told her I didn't mind if they explored something—though, admittedly, Jax was never interested. "You know I don't care, right? If you want to go for it, go ahead. But if things go south, I can't be caught in the middle."

She chews on her bottom lip, nodding slowly.

With a slight giggle, she changes the subject. "Did you see how Damien looked at you?"

I sigh, nodding but staying silent. I couldn't bring myself to voice the storm of thoughts swirling in my head.

While we wait, we experiment with different styles for Amara's hair. We tried a few, but they're too elaborate and distracted from the dress. In the end, we settle on a simple, low, messy bun. Just as we're finishing up, the doorbell rings.

"I'll get it," I say. Amara tells me she'll finish up her hair and join me once she's done.

I head downstairs and open the door—then freeze.

"Jake?" I gasp, my hand gripping the door harder.

He rakes his eyes over me with a bold smirk, and suddenly, I feel exposed in my dress.

"Damn, baby, you look sexy as fuck," he purrs.

I fight the urge to scream or cry. Instead, I raise my chin, forcing confidence into my voice. "I know."

I glance past him. "I'm surprised you could pull your dick out of Tina long enough to apologize." I put my hand on my hip, summoning the strength to stand firm for at least five minutes.

He chuckles—a sound that makes my blood boil. His outfit is simple: a black sweater, jeans, boots, and a black beanie. A couple of months ago, I would have been throwing myself at him, drawn in by the sight of wisps of blonde hair curling out of the beanie, the contrast of his dark clothes against his striking blue eyes. But not anymore.

"Oh, that," he says, his voice smooth. "I'm sorry, baby. She didn't mean anything. It was a mistake." He steps forward, but I don't move.

I scoff. "A mistake, huh? I'm sure it's one you've made many times." I roll my eyes at his ridiculous toxic masculinity.

He reaches for me, and I step back, holding up my hand to stop him from touching me.

"You're right. I was wrong," he says, voice softening. "They meant nothing to me. I see that now. I was just scared we were getting serious, and I panicked. My parents were talking about marriage, and I freaked, okay? But I'm good now. I've gotten it out of my system." He reaches for me again, his voice filled with false sincerity.

I stare at him in disbelief. "*They?* As in more than one?" I ask, and he nods, unashamed.

"You're a fucking asshole," I spit. "We were together for three years, and because your parents talked about marriage, you think you need to stick your tiny dick in every willing girl?"

He shrugs like it was no big deal.

"It's not like that, baby. It was only three-okay, four girls. But it's in the past. I'm ready to be what you need now." He takes another step toward me.

I shake my head, anger boiling over. "The only thing I need from you is to leave. *Now*."

I move to shut the door, but he shoves it open and grabs my arm, pulling me toward him.

"What happened to the girl who threw herself at me every chance she got?" he asks, spinning us around and pinning me to the doorframe.

I shove at his chest, but he doesn't budge. "The only reason I threw myself at you was because I was never fully satisfied," I hiss.

He leans down, pressing his lips to my neck before trailing his nose up to my jaw. Then he kisses my jaw and moves to capture my lips. When I shove him harder, he catches my lips. I freeze—I can't move. I seal my lips tight, suppressing the gag that rises when he licks at them.

I can't believe I used to be with this piece of shit.

When I don't kiss him back, he pulls away, shock written all over his face, as if no woman has ever denied him. He thought he would win me back, that a shitty excuse and a sloppy kiss would pull me back to him.

The truth is, he's not even a good kisser—not even mediocre. He's a licker, with no control or a hint of mastery.

"Are you seeing someone else? Is that what this is?" he sneers, gesturing to my dress.

My confusion must be obvious on my face, because his next words cut deeper than they should.

"Are you such a slut that you move on to the next guy who shows you attention? Is that what this dress is for? Did you think your new man was at the door?" His words hang in the air like a slap.

I shake off the confusion, refusing to let him get under my skin. He doesn't have that kind of influence over me anymore. "*No*. Unlike you, I can control myself. Not that I owe you an explanation, but

Amara and I are just trying on dresses for the weekend. We're going to a Christmas party together." I try to put distance between us, taking a step back.

Just then, Amara calls from inside the house. "I think I got the hair figured out for the party!" she says, her voice light and excited. She rounds the corner in her dress, rolling her eyes. "Who dragged up the trash?"

Jake tries to pull me closer, but I immediately yank myself free. "I was just coming to make up with Anastasia," he says, his tone defensive.

I step back, my anger rising. "You were just leaving. We're done. You cheated, more than once, over things that didn't even matter," I hiss, resentment dripping in my tone. "I never saw us getting married, anyway, so stop using that as some excuse. You're just a shitty person."

The bitch in me surfaces with every word, growing more forceful.

"Fine," he huffs out, a sneer that truly belongs on his face making its appearance. "But when you finally realize you can't do better than me, don't expect me to be waiting." He turns on his heel and stalks off.

I shout after him, the need to have the last word burning through me. "I could do better than you, even if I end up alone with just my toy!"

Amara bursts into laughter behind me, clearly entertained by my comment.

I slam the door behind me, seething with anger, but the satisfaction of sending him off with his tail between his legs fuels me. It doesn't matter anymore. I have two men who seem to want me. One knows how to please me, while the other knows how to push my buttons and get under my skin in ways no other man ever has.

I don't need him—frankly, I never have.

Him

Watching my brother touch her made my blood boil. She said no—anyone with eyes could see how uncomfortable she was. And yet, he still touched her, as if he had some kind of claim on her, as if he was entitled.

When he finally leaves, I glance at her one last time. My little angel. That stunning green dress clings to her in a way that makes it nearly impossible to look away. But I force myself to. With more effort than I'd like to admit, I turn and follow him.

We need to have a conversation about his behavior.

Her

With a sigh, I throw off the covers and groan. The events of the night refused to let me rest, leaving me tossing and turning. After Jake left, Amara tried her best to cheer me up, but it didn't take her long to notice I needed to be alone. Glancing at the clock, the bright red numbers glare back at me: 4:30 a.m. At the rate my mind is racing, I know there's no chance of falling back asleep.

Resigned, I slip on a pair of sweatpants and my fluffy robe, hunting for my equally fluffy slippers to complete the ensemble. Once I'm bundled up and somewhat comfortable, I shuffle downstairs to the kitchen.

The couch is empty, confirming Damien isn't here to get under my skin today—a small mercy. I don't have the energy to deal with him, and I doubt it would end well if I tried. Dragging my feet across the floor, I locate my favorite coffee mug and pull out the ingredients for peppermint hot chocolate—my go-to comfort drink. To top it off, I add a candy cane to use as a stirrer.

With the warm mug in hand, I head toward the living room but hesitate. Instead, I step outside to sit on the porch swing. The crisp air hits me the moment I step onto the stoop, and I take a deep breath, letting it awaken me even more. My eyes wander to the mailbox, but for the second day in a row, there's no sign of a gift waiting for me. This time, though, the disappointment I feel doesn't catch me off guard. I already checked my phone earlier—no message there either.

Sighing, I shuffle to the swing and sit, cradling my mug. I take a sip, the warmth wrapping around my soul like a hug. The heat seeps through my palms, grounding me as my thoughts start to wander. Unfortunately, they don't take long to turn against me.

I wonder, *what's wrong with me?* What could make Jake cheat? Even though I never saw a real future with him, the memory of his confession stabs at my heart: Four. He cheated on me with *four* other women. I always thought Jake was the safe choice, the guy who'd never hurt me. I huff out a bitter laugh. A lot of good that did.

The steam from my mug curls into the chilled air, swirling in mesmerizing patterns. It's calming in a way, but not enough to quell the storm raging inside me. Sadness and hurt morph into anger and frustration in a relentless cycle. Looking back now, the signs were there—the excuses, the late nights, the lies. I just didn't want to see them. I thought he was safe, but he was anything but.

And I refuse to let him bring me down anymore.

Anger flares hot in my chest—not at him, but at myself. For letting him make me feel like I wasn't enough. *He cheated; I didn't force him to.* Growling in frustration, I yank the candy cane from my mug and hurl it onto the porch. It shatters, scattering pieces across the stoop.

For a moment, I stare at the mess. The candy cane looks like it exploded, fragments scattering far and wide. My eyes trace the pieces until they land on something else—a small box sitting near one of the porch columns.

My breath catches.

The familiar packaging, the neatly tied red bow—it's just like the last one. The one from my mystery man. The one that came with photos of me sprawled out for him, wearing his cum-stained shirt.

Heart pounding, I rush forward to grab the box, barely pausing long enough to discard the rest of my drink in the sink before sprinting upstairs to my room.

Excitement thrums through me, my earlier worries forgotten like the shattered candy cane left outside. Once in my room, I sit cross-legged on the bed and open the box.

The first thing I see is the note. I pull it out carefully, my fingers trembling. But as I read, confusion clouds my excitement, twisting it into something else entirely.

'Only I get to touch you, little angel. Let this be your first and last warning. When you're ready, let me know, and I will pleasure you in ways you could only imagine.'

The note sends a chill down my spine. He was there. Watching when Jake kissed me. That thought alone has me scrubbing the back of my hand across my lips, as though I could wipe away the slimy memory of Jake's tongue. *Nasty.*

My gaze falls on the small bag inside the box. I hesitate, a flicker of unease creeping in. I've read enough dark romance to know that when an unhinged man starts sending you gifts, nothing good usually comes of it. Steeling myself, I take a deep breath and prepare for whatever twisted surprise he might've left for me.

When I finally opened the bag, the breath I didn't realize I was holding whooshes out of me. Then I laugh nervously. It's definitely *not* a body part. It's...a sex toy.

Curiosity turns into confusion as I examine it more closely. I wanted Jake to try something like this once. A remote-controlled toy to spice things up. But as I look again, I realize there's no remote—not in the bag, not in the box. I check twice. My eyes fall back to the note:

'Let me know when you're ready.'

Grinning despite myself, I grab my phone and pull up the unknown contact. My fingers hover over the screen before I type:

> Nice toy. But you forgot the remote.

I hit send before I can second-guess myself. As I sit there, staring at the message, I read it over and over, biting my thumbnail—a nervous habit I can't seem to break. Minutes tick by, but there's no response. It's barely five in the morning; my mystery man is probably asleep. With a dramatic sigh, I toss myself backward onto the bed and scream into the heart-shaped pillow Amara gave me when we were twelve.

Lying there, doubts creep in. Maybe my message was too bratty. Maybe he's into the idea of me, not the real me. What if—

My phone vibrates. Heart racing, I scramble to grab it.

> I *am* the remote, little angel.

I roll my eyes, letting out an exasperated breath. Seriously? My reply is instant:

> Is that supposed to do something for me?

The response comes almost immediately, making me smile despite myself.

> Try it out and see exactly what it can do for you, little angel.

The thought stirs my curiosity, but I won't give in that easily. *Why?* I type, smirking as I press send.

> Why? I have toys that will get me off just fine.

As soon as my message is marked as read, a video chat request pops up. I decline it, my stubbornness kicking in. Instead, I grab one of my vibrators from my nightstand, discarding my robe and sweatpants in the process. Settling back on the bed, I position the toy at my entrance and hit record on my phone.

The smooth silicone breaches me, and I moan, sliding it in deeper and deeper until it's buried fully inside me. Slowly, I pull it out, then thrust it back in hard. The mix of pleasure and pain makes my back arch off the bed as a louder moan escapes my lips. My phone vibrates with another call, but I decline it again. Then again.

> If you know what's good for you, you'll answer the goddamn phone, Anastasia. Now.

Smirking, I quickly type back:

> I'm busy, and you keep interrupting me.

I attach the short video clip of me fucking myself and press send. His response is instant.

> Fuck, you're such a fucking brat.

> As good as you look stuffing that toy in your pretty pussy, I still think mine would look better.

His words send a rush of heat through me. My fingers hover over the screen before I type back:

> And what's so special about your toy?

The reply is swift and taunting:

> I dare you to find out.

> You answer, and I'll talk you through it.

As tempted as I am, I won't give in so easily. My defiance kicks in once more.

> And what do I get if you can't make me cum?

The typing indicator appears, disappears, then reappears. The cycle has me biting my thumbnail in anticipation. Finally, his response comes through, and it steals the breath from my lungs.

> Me. You get me, little angel. I'll reveal myself to you today.

> On one condition: when I make you cum—and mark my words, I will—you'll play my little game until Christmas Eve. I'll do whatever I want to you, whenever I want.

> Do we have a deal?

I freeze. Part of me wants to know who he is, to finally put a face to the unknown man, but I refuse to give in so easily. A smirk curls my lips as I whisper, "Challenge accepted."

Then I type my reply:

> You can try.

That's all the invitation he needs to call me again. This time, I don't deny the call—but I don't answer it right away either. Letting him wait gives me the smallest sliver of control in this game. The only reason I agreed was because curiosity got the best of me.

Finally, I answer. "Hello, mystery man," I purr, keeping my camera off for now.

"Hello, little angel." His voice is low, deep, almost a whisper. The way his words slide through the phone feels intimate, like he's deliberately hiding his voice from me, drawing me in. The sound alone sends shivers down my spine.

"Are you ready for our little game?" he asks.

I let a deliberate pause stretch between us. Slowly, I move, making sure he can hear the soft rustle of my shirt sliding off. Only then do I turn on the camera, angling it so the first thing he sees is my bare chest.

The groan that escapes him makes me smile.

"Fuck," he growls, his voice thick with desire. "You're even more perfect than I imagined."

I lean back against my pillows, positioning myself so he can see the toy in my hand. "Shall we start?" I say, a teasing edge to my voice. "And when you finally reveal yourself, make sure you're ready to make it up to me."

He chuckles, a deep, rumbling sound that makes my core clench. "Are you ready to listen?" he counters.

I shrug, feigning nonchalance. "I'll try. No promises."

"I expect nothing less from you," he replies lowly, amusement lacing his tone. "Now, turn it on. Slide it in—slowly. Prop your phone up so I can watch you."

I move like I'm about to obey but pause, tilting my head in mock defiance. "Don't I get to see something? Anything, while I do this?"

"That wasn't part of the deal, now was it?" he asks, his voice firm.

I want to argue, to push him, but I already know he's right. If I press too hard, I risk him calling it all off, and that's a gamble I'm not willing to take. For now.

Instead, I move my phone, propping it up on the same pillow I screamed into earlier. He watches as I guide the toy to my entrance, taking my time. "Look at how nicely that pussy takes my toy," he murmurs, the emphasis on the word *my* not lost on me.

Once the toy is fully seated, one arm resting against my clit and the other nestled firmly against my g-spot, I wait. The anticipation builds with every second of silence.

Finally, his voice cuts through the quiet. "See, this toy is special. I control the vibrations. I decide how strong they feel..."

A sudden jolt against my clit makes me gasp, a deep moan slipping from my lips.

"...how long they last," he continues, and another pulse vibrates through me, this one so intense it shoots straight to my core. My hips buck involuntarily, grinding against the invisible force of pleasure.

"That's it, angel," he praises, his voice like a velvet caress. "Work those hips for me. I'm right here with you. Listen."

His words anchor me, and I force myself to focus, straining to hear what he wants me to notice.

"What do you hear?" he asks, his tone dark, commanding.

At first, I don't register it, too caught up in the sensations rolling through my body. But then, faintly, I catch it—the rhythmic, unmistakable sound of him pleasuring himself.

"You," I breathe, my voice trembling. "I hear you pleasuring yourself."

"Good girl," he says, his voice dripping with satisfaction.

"That's right. I'm so fucking hard for you, it hurts," he admits, his voice a raw whisper. His words drag a needy whimper from my lips, one I can't suppress.

"Now," he commands, his tone dark and breathless. "Show me how you want me to touch you."

My hand moves instinctively, cupping my breasts, fingers teasing the sensitive peaks. It's a slow, deliberate game I play, testing his patience as much as my own. He lets me continue, watching—or listening—intently as I touch, tease, and pinch my nipples. I lose myself in the act, one hand tangling in my hair, tugging slightly. The other pinches hard, pulling my nipple just to the edge of pain.

When his voice breaks the silence, it's not a command—it's a moan. My name spills from his lips like a prayer, reverberating in my chest and making my back arch as I crest a peak of pleasure. But it's not enough. I need more.

I focus on the steady rhythm of his hand on himself, the slick, rhythmic sound pushing me closer to madness.

"Do you want to know why I chose this toy for you?" he murmurs, his voice like liquid silk.

A desperate whimper escapes me in response, my lips too busy biting back the need building inside me to form words.

"That's all I needed to hear," he continues, his tone smug and dripping with control. "You see, this toy has a special feature. It takes sound—specific frequencies—and turns them into vibrations."

For a moment, the toy goes still, and I gasp at the sudden loss. The whine that escapes me is pure desperation, a sound I'd never meant for him to hear.

"Patience," he soothes, and I can hear the smile in his voice. "I promise, it's worth it."

When the vibrations resume, they're nothing like before. The pulses are erratic—some soft and teasing, others sudden and strong, each one unpredictable. They play against me, testing my limits, building me up and holding me back all at once. I try to focus on the chaotic rhythm, but his voice is impossible to ignore.

"Keep touching yourself," he orders, the silkiness of his tone sending a fresh wave of heat coursing through me.

My hand tightens in my hair, the pull grounding me as my other hand moves to massage my chest roughly. The tension in my gut coils tighter, my body trembling on the edge of release. But it's not enough—*I need more.*

"Is that all you've got?" I challenge breathlessly, though the trembling in my voice betrays my bravado.

That damn chuckle of his fills the silence, light yet dark, soft yet oppressive. His laughter feels like shadowed hands sliding over my body, pulling me under, a darkness I can't help but crave.

"Well," he breathes, his strokes slowing. He's waiting, holding back, no doubt savoring my impending surrender. "I don't share, angel. I don't take it well when someone touches what's mine. Like your good-for-nothing ex."

My resolve flares at his words, sharp and defiant. "I am not yours," I snap, my voice stronger than I feel.

But even as I say it—*I am not his, I am not his, I am not his*—the mantra crumbles in my mind. Each pulse between my thighs chips away at my resistance.

I cling to that flicker of defiance like a lifeline, hoping it will keep the waves of pleasure at bay. But deep down, I already know the truth. That flame of rebellion will be drowned, swallowed whole by the tide he's pulling me into.

The sound of flesh meeting flesh grows louder, and his voice drops into a low groan. "It's cute you think that. But from where I'm sitting, your body hasn't gotten the message."

Fuck, he's right. I'm a writhing, needy mess for him—and he hasn't even touched me yet.

A deep, guttural moan tears from my throat as my back arches. "Fuck, I'm close. More," I demand, the edge of desperation lacing my voice.

He gasps softly, almost like he's feeling every ounce of tension I am. His words slip through the haze of my pleasure, shoving me closer to the brink. "I guess I should mention... After he left, I followed him," he says darkly.

What?

"And I beat the ever-loving shit out of him for touching you."

The words barely register. I'm too high, too close to the edge, to fully process what he's saying. All I know is that his rough growl is sending shockwaves through me, pushing me toward the precipice. My free hand moves instinctively, wrapping around my throat, squeezing gently as I moan louder.

"Cum with me," he demands harshly.

That's it. That's all it takes. My body erupts, my back bowing off the bed as I scream into my arm to muffle the sound.

"Fuck!" The word is ripped from me, raw and broken, as my legs tighten and my toes curl. Pleasure crashes through me like a tidal wave, leaving me trembling.

Through the haze of my orgasm, I hear his breathing grow ragged, hear the slick, frantic rhythm of his hand. He's close too, riding the same edge, trying to prolong his release.

"Spread those pretty fucking thighs," he growls, his voice thick and commanding. "I want to see what *I* did to you."

My entire body protests, trembling and oversensitive, but I do as he says, forcing my legs open. The toy still hums mercilessly against me, making me twitch.

"Now, take it out," he orders. "Show me how much you came for me."

The overstimulation is unbearable, but I obey, pulling the toy free.

"Shit, little angel," he murmurs, a low groan escaping him. "You made a mess."

His praise sends a new wave of heat coursing through me. Fueled by a need to leave him as wrecked as I am, I sit up slowly. My gaze locked on the camera, I bring the toy to my lips and slide it into my mouth. The tangy sweetness of my release coats my tongue, and I moan softly for him.

He groans again, a desperate, strained sound. "You'll be the death of me."

I let the toy slip from my mouth and set it aside, watching him, waiting for his next move.

But then his voice drops, laced with a dark satisfaction. "Oh, and there's one thing I didn't tell you."

I freeze, my full attention snapping to his words. I can hear the smirk in his voice—he knows he's won this game.

"I recorded myself beating your pathetic ex," he says, his tone very matter of fact. "And those sounds? The ones you just got off to. That's what they were."

My mouth opens, then closes. I don't know what to say.

"Have a good day, little angel," he purrs. "I'll be seeing you soon."

The line goes dead before I can respond, leaving me sitting there in stunned silence.

I don't know how to feel about his admission. That's a lie—I know exactly how I feel. I just refuse to name the emotions swirling in my chest. I should feel ashamed. But shame isn't what's coiling through me.

The thought of what just happened, of the power he holds over me, plays on a loop in my mind. A small, dark part of me liked it. No—relished it.

I know this is only the beginning. Over the next week, he'll feed this hunger in me, coaxing it to grow. And I'll let him. I'll crave it.

Finally feeling satisfied—more so because it wasn't by my own hand—I clean up, put the toy away, and crawl back into bed.

As I drift off, I can't help but wonder what he looks like. Who the man behind the voice, the control, the darkness truly is.

Him

After hanging up with my little angel, a low laugh escapes me, echoing in the quiet room. Her surprise at my little omission was everything I hoped for. She wasn't upset—that much was obvious—but the look on her face lingers in my mind, and I can't quite decide how to feel about it.

One thing is certain: I wasn't kidding when I said I don't share. It was hard enough watching my brother with her over the last few years, knowing she didn't see me the way I saw her. The way I wanted her to see me.

But now? Now, I have my chance.

Winning our little bet is just the beginning, though. If I'm going to make good on my promises over the next eight nights, I have some planning to do. Ideas are already churning in my head, each one more tantalizing than the last. But above all else, I need her consent. Without it, none of this means anything.

The memory of her shattering for me, the way she came so beautifully, is burned into my brain. I crave it again. The sounds she made—the moans, the gasps, the desperate edge in her voice—play on a loop in my head. Just the thought of it has my dick stirring to life again, even though I just came harder than I ever have in my life.

Groaning in frustration, I push myself out of bed and head to the bathroom. I need a cold shower. Badly.

Under the icy spray, I let out a deep breath, trying to cool the heat coursing through my veins. It's futile, though. No amount of cold water can stop the fire that's burning in me, fueled by thoughts of her. Of what I'll do to her next.

I know her. I know that no matter how much she mouths off to me, no matter how much she pretends to fight, this is what she wants. I am what she wants.

And I'll give her exactly what she needs.

Her

I felt conflicted all day. On one hand, I should feel guilty, ashamed, or even embarrassed that I got off to the sounds of my stalker beating my ex. But on the other hand, it was the first time I'd ever come at the hands of someone else.

After a few hours of distracted cleaning and reorganizing my library, I realized my thoughts kept circling back to him. I imagined all the things he might do to me if he were with me in person. It didn't help that I was shelving books I'd already read, and with a few of them, vivid scenes came to mind—scenes I wouldn't mind acting out.

New fantasies kept bubbling up, ideas I hadn't even realized I wanted. Because, after everything, I knew he'd be open to it. But fantasizing about a masked man isn't normal. Eventually, I tried to escape my thoughts by reading, but I couldn't focus. So, I went downstairs to watch TV, where I ended up falling asleep.

I wake to the sensation of my feet being moved. Groggy, I open my eyes to find chocolate-brown ones staring back at me.

"I didn't mean to wake you, but you were taking up the whole couch," Damien says softly, sitting down and placing my feet in his lap.

Stretching, I ask, "What time is it?"

He doesn't answer right away, his gaze catching on my bare stomach. My shirt has ridden up in my sleep, and the stretch only makes it worse. His attention lingers on the strip of skin, and I become acutely aware of just how cropped my shirt is—it's barely covering the underside of my breasts.

I smirk. It wasn't often I managed to get this kind of reaction from him. "Take a picture; it'll last longer," I tease, repeating his own words from a couple of mornings ago.

I don't expect him to actually pull out his phone.

"Damien!" I yelp, scrambling to cover myself. But in my panic, I manage to tug my shirt up even higher, flashing him completely.

Adjusting himself in his pants, he smirks. "You'd look hot as fuck with your tits pierced."

I scoff, my face heating as I finally manage to pull my shirt down. I act like nothing happened, especially when Jaxson walks into the room. I sit up, giving him room on the couch, and he remains blissfully oblivious to the tension crackling between his baby sister and his best friend.

Three more days. I only have to make it through three more days before I can get away. Three days, and I'll finally have some fun without Damien breathing down my neck, driving me insane, and leaving me on edge. Then, I'll have my mystery man—someone who seems to know my darkest desires—ready to make them come true.

The doorbell rings, and Jaxson mentions he's ordered food. Grateful for the distraction, I jump up, desperate for some space from the tattooed god currently consuming half my thoughts.

When I opened the door for the delivery, I notice a small box with a red bow tucked into the bag. My heart skips.

"Your foods in the kitchen," I call to Jaxson, rushing upstairs to my room with the mysterious package in hand.

Part of me hates how excited I get when I find one of his gifts. I guess I hate how much I've come to depend not just on the gifts, but on him too. And knowing that he has this "game" planned for me over the next seven nights fills me with equal parts excitement and irritation.

I don't like feeling out of control. Yet, at the same time, I crave it. I crave surrendering, giving up my choices, and letting someone else take what they want from me. For some reason, my mystery man feels like the type who would take everything I had to offer—and more—but he'd give just as much in return.

It's becoming clear that he's in this for more than I anticipated. But that's not something I'm ready to think too deeply about right now. All I want is to see what he's left for me.

A jolt of anxiety shoots through me as I sit on my bed, staring at the little brown box resting on my emerald quilt. I don't know what I agreed to. I didn't realize, when I said yes to him, how thoroughly he'd play my body—and my mind.

With my knees crossed, I stare at the box a little longer, holding off. There's always a rush of excitement when I open these gifts, but I never know what to expect. Finally, I tug the red bow loose, lift the lid, and peek inside.

At first, I have no idea what I'm looking at. It seems to be a roll of duct tape—but it's hot pink. When I pick it up, though, it doesn't feel like duct tape. It's lighter, softer, and doesn't stick to my fingers. There's also a black blindfold tucked beneath it.

I find the note tucked underneath the blindfold. It reads:

This one is more for me, but don't worry, little angel, I promise to make sure you enjoy it too.

What the actual fuck? How is this for him? Am I supposed to tie him up? A twisted smile curls my lips at the thought. I'd love to take control of him for once—to flip the script and make him feel as vulnerable as he makes me feel.

A little more inspection reveals two things: first, the tape isn't adhesive—it only sticks to itself. And second, it's very clear he plans to use it to tie *me* up.

The realization sends a pulsing heat straight to my clit, and my empty core clenches around nothing. The thought pisses me off—though I'd never admit what he does to me, not even to myself.

I know he's expecting me to reach out after our conversation last night, expecting me to tell him what I think of his little gift. But I also know I'll get a bigger reaction if I don't.

After all, I haven't been sleeping well since the whole Jake fiasco.

Smiling to myself, I set the tape on my nightstand, slip on a nightgown, and crawl into bed. After plugging my phone in and setting it to silent, I close my eyes. Sleep comes easily, though my thoughts linger on my mystery man. He doesn't just tolerate the brattiness that others have tried to stifle in me—he seems to enjoy it. He lets me push, tease, and provoke him until he snaps, and I can't help but love it when he does.

He knows how to put me in my place.

And I have a feeling that, given the chance, he's going to do just that.

I wake to the sensation of something wrapping around my wrist. Before I can make a sound, a strong, gloved hand clamps over my mouth.

"You thought I wouldn't come?" his voice rumbles in the darkness.

My world is pitch black; thanks to the blindfold he's put over my eyes. I glare in his direction—not that he can see—but deep down, I'm not disappointed. He's done exactly what I'd hoped he would.

When he's sure I won't scream, he removes his hand.

"Took you long enough," I say, feigning nonchalance.

He chuckles, a low, deep sound that sends a shiver down my spine. "I know what you're playing at, little angel. But it's my game now."

His breath ghosts against my ear as he speaks, and before I can reply, his teeth graze my earlobe. He sucks it into his mouth, his tongue flicking over the sensitive skin.

Heat rushes to my core, and I arch into him instinctively, wishing it were another part of me in his mouth.

A low moan escapes my lips, and I tip my head back, giving him full access to my neck. He takes it, kissing, nipping, and sucking his way down the column of my throat.

When he reaches my collarbone, my skin erupts into goosebumps, and my breath hitches.

He slips his hand under my nightgown, ghosting his touch over my ribcage. The sensation sends a shudder of pleasure through me. Pinning my restrained hands above my head, he whispers, "You think you were being cute tonight, don't you?" His other hand grips my breast almost painfully, and he pinches my nipple, coaxing another moan from me.

He presses his hips into mine, pinning me to the bed and forcing my thighs to accommodate his hard body. "Well, we'll see how cute you think it is when I have you so worked up that you beg me to let you come. But when I finally do, your body will be so overworked and used that it won't let you."

I roll my hips into him, pressing back against his hardness. "I wasn't trying to be cute," I moan. "I was trying to get your attention."

At my admission, he groans, rocking into me, rubbing his hard length against my aching core through the fabric. "You always have my attention, little angel," he growls.

His words stir something deep in my chest—something unfamiliar. With my ex, I had to fight for his attention, his time, his affection. He'd always promise to try harder, but he never did, and then we'd end up fighting. But with my mystery man, I know I won't have to fight for any of that. It should scare me, but it doesn't. It thrills me to know this man is so consumed by me that not sending him a single text today has him pinning me to the bed, bound and vulnerable, ready to be used as he sees fit.

The thought makes me whimper. He takes my restrained hands and pins them above my head. "Be a good girl for me, keep your hands where they are, and I might just let you come."

His words drive me mad. I want to defy him, to see what he'll do if I don't listen. When his hand releases mine, I immediately move them, instinctively testing him. But he's ready. His hand is there in an instant, forcing my hands back into the mattress while his other slaps my breast.

I gasp, then moan. "This is your last warning, little angel. Keep your hands there. Don't move them."

I can hear the smile in his voice, like he knew exactly what I'd do. He expected me to move, to defy him. "You look so cute when you get bratty."

His words piss me off. How can he read me so well? How long has he been watching me? Why wait? I know he's not afraid of my ex if last night's events are any indication. So why now?

The feeling of my shirt being pushed up to expose my breasts to him makes my breath hitch. I don't know what to expect, or where he'll touch me next. Feeling so completely out of control of the situation is new to me, but the idea of relinquishing control, of letting him take charge, has me melting into the mattress.

The thought of proving him wrong keeps me obedient. I leave my hands exactly where he wants them, the pulse of excitement overwhelming any desire to rebel.

Him

Having my little angel bound beneath me has every muscle in my body straining for control. The tight pull of my black jeans is a distraction, but nothing compared to the sight of her laid out before me. I had a feeling she ignored me today just to provoke me, to get a reaction. But it never occurred to me she might crave my attention this much. A part of me hates that she feels she has to fight for it—as though she's not already my every waking thought.

An irritated whimper pulls me from my thoughts. To my surprise, she hasn't moved her hands, though I half-expected her to. I'd planned to tease her, to leave her on edge until she'd think of nothing but me long after I was gone. But her obedience is steadfast, and for that, I'll reward her in the sweetest torment—holding her on that fine edge for as long as I can before finally letting her fall. When she does, I'll be there to catch her, to pick up the pieces and put her back together again.

I push her nightgown higher, ensuring it stays in place just above her breasts. The soft fabric clings to her curves, but I don't want it getting in my way. Her chest rises and falls, her nipples tightening under the faint brush of my gloved fingers. The temptation is too much. I lean down, capturing one of those hardened peaks in my mouth, my teeth grazing lightly. She arches into me, gasping when I bite down just enough to test her limits. The sharp intake of breath, the way her hips grind against me—it's all the encouragement I need.

Slowly, I explore her body, learning what makes her gasp, moan, and writhe. My hands and mouth map the sensitive curves of her breasts, teasing her with the bite of pain followed by the soothing stroke of a caress. The contrast leaves her trembling, her reactions a symphony of pleasure and need. She moans louder when I suck the tender underside of her breast, and I leave a mark there—a reminder for me, and for anyone else who might see it, though the latter thought stirs a possessive fire in me.

Without thinking, I rip her panties down her thighs, pressing them against her stomach before delivering a sharp slap to her slick heat. "This pussy is mine," I growl, my voice rough with need. Her moan is louder now, her hands still obediently in place. She's enjoying this as much as I am.

But I need her to understand—no one else can bring her to the brink like I can. No one else will ever know her the way I do. That thought drives me mad, and control slips further from my grasp.

I shove two gloved fingers into her tight pussy, curling them to find the spot deep inside that I know no one else has ever touched. My other hand covers her mouth, muffling her cries as her hips move in perfect rhythm with mine. "Fuck, yes," she moans into my hand, her desperation fueling me.

When I press my thumb to her clit, she clenches hard around my fingers, her body teetering on the edge. But I pull back before she can tip over, withdrawing both my hand and fingers. "Not so fast, little angel," I say, delivering another sharp slap to her swollen clit. Her body jolts, curses spilling from her lips.

Her hips buck forward, seeking friction. "Fuck you," she spits angrily, her voice shaking. "I knew you couldn't get me off. I'll just do it myself."

I click my tongue, shaking my head. "Ah, ah. Remember the rules. If you move, I'll keep you like this all night—so worked up your body won't know how to finish." My words have the intended effect; she freezes, her hands still obediently in place.

Leaning over her trembling body, I slide my fingers back into her, thrusting just as brutally as before. Her walls pulse around me, her breathing ragged. Her chest rises and falls, her nipples taut as I reach out to squeeze one. My mouth finds the soft skin of her inner thigh, biting and sucking until her moans turn into cries.

"Fuck, I'm going to—" The words die in her throat as I pull away again, leaving her panting and on the brink of frustration.

I chuckle darkly, watching her writhe. "You'll learn your lesson tonight, little angel."

Her glare is sharp, it cuts through her covered eyes, but the tremor in her voice betrays her. "I'm beginning to think you don't know what you're doing," she taunts, though the tremble in her voice tells me otherwise.

Moving up her body, I slide her panties the rest of the way off, savoring the smooth glide of fabric over her skin. Then I press myself against her, making sure she feels how hard I am as I rock into her, slow and deliberate. Her breath catches, but I lean in close, my lips brushing her ear.

"I know what you're doing," I murmur, my voice low and rough. "But it won't work. My only thought right now is to show you that I'm the only one who can get you off—not to please you. I started wanting to, but now?" I grind into her, letting her feel my need. "Now, the need to claim you—all of you—has become too much. So, you'll learn."

She starts moving against me, seeking her own rhythm, and I let her, watching the way she loses herself to the friction. My mouth trails down her neck, licking and nibbling at the sensitive skin. Her breath hitches when I move lower, my lips finding her breasts again.

I've already brought her to the edge more than once, and now I see the signs—her body trembling, her thighs pressing together, the slight arch of her back. She tries to hide it, but I know better. Smirking, I pull away just as she's on the brink.

"Where are your toys?" I ask, a new idea flickering to life.

She lets out a ragged breath, her frustration evident. "In the drawer... next to the bed."

It takes me no time to find what I'm looking for—a silicone toy that's just the right size. Holding it in my hand, I glance back at her, laid bare and trembling. I want to bury myself in her, to feel her tighten around me, but I've already decided she won't get that—not yet. Not until she knows it's me she craves, and only if she truly wants it. For now, my hands and this toy will do.

Because I know... once I'm inside her, there will be no going back.

With the toy in one hand, I sit back on my knees and free my cock from my jeans, her soft whimper shooting straight to my core. The way she moans when I slide the toy into her dripping pussy has me gripping my shaft, stroking in time with the slow, deliberate rhythm I set for her.

"That's right," I say, my voice thick with desire. "Take that fucking cock." Her moans grow louder, and I know she likes hearing me talk just as much as I like watching her. "Fuck, baby, you're so tight."

The toy isn't as big as me, and yet she's stretching to take it. The sight of her makes my cock throb in my hand, and I can't help but imagine how it would feel to be inside her, buried deep.

She starts whimpering, her body trembling beneath me. "Please," she gasps, her voice desperate. "I'm so close. Please let me cum—I need you."

That last admission sends a shiver down my spine, and I find myself pumping the toy harder, matching the pace with my own hand.

"You've been such a good girl for me," I pant, my breath coming in short bursts. "I can't deny you what you need." My body tenses, the heat building low in my belly as I watch her come undone. "Only I can give you what you need."

Her head falls back, her lip caught between her teeth as she tries to hold back a scream. Her legs start to shake, pressing together as her orgasm builds.

"Shit," she breathes, her voice breaking. "I'm going to cum."

I'm on the edge myself, the tingling heat racing down my spine. I press the toy in as deep as it can go, my palm against its base, and use my thumb to circle her clit. That's all it takes to send her spiraling over the edge. She screams into her arm, her body arching as waves of pleasure roll through her.

Her cries, the way her body clenches around the toy—it's too much. I stroke myself faster, groaning as my own release hits. Thick ropes spill over my hand, the toy, and her clit, mixing with the wetness already there.

"Fuck, little angel," I moan, my voice rough with satisfaction. "The things you do to me."

She gasps, her head turning in my direction, her chest still heaving. "Did you just...?" She trails off, but the question lingers between us.

"Yes," I murmur, my thumb gliding over her sensitive clit, smearing my release against her, silently wishing it was inside of her instead. "Do you feel it? Right here?" Her moans, softer now, tell me all I need to know.

"Do you like that?" I ask, watching her closely.

Her breath catches, and she nods, her voice barely above a whisper. "Yes."

"Noted," I say with a smirk, pulling the toy out of her. I tuck myself back into my jeans, my mind replaying the way she came so beautifully for me. But I missed it—the look on her face as she fell apart, my focus was elsewhere.

Next time, I'll make sure I see everything.

She's melted into the mattress, her body completely relaxed. The soft, contented sigh that escapes her lips tells me everything I need to know—I've accomplished exactly what I set out to do. Next time she's alone, craving release, she'll think of this moment. She'll remember how I worked her body in ways no one else ever could.

A satisfied smirk tugs at my lips as I rise from the bed and head to the bathroom, grabbing a warm rag to clean her up. When I return, her slow, even breaths tell me she's already drifted off to sleep. The sight of her, so peaceful and vulnerable, stirs something deep within me, but I push it aside. She can't know who I am—not yet.

Carefully, I clean her up, my hands gentle and deliberate. Once finished, I untie her wrists, making sure to move quietly so I don't wake her. The faint marks on her skin make me pause, and for a moment, I trace them with my fingers. A part of me wants to stay, but I know better. There's still more to this game.

Leaning down, I press a soft kiss to the top of her head, breathing in her scent one last time before pulling back. She stirs slightly but doesn't wake, her body curling into the warmth of the sheets.

Glancing at the clock, I note it's only about ten. The store I need to visit should still be open. With one last look at her sleeping form—so beautifully wrecked and utterly mine—I slip out of the room, closing the door quietly behind me.

The night isn't over yet.

Her

I woke late in the morning, feeling clean, untied, and wrapped snugly under the covers. My body felt sore, but in the best way. Memories of last night played through my mind in vivid detail. At first, he'd been slow and deliberate, every touch calculated to draw out my pleasure. Then, without warning, he shifted—possessive, rough, and completely consuming.

I won't deny it—I liked it.

The way he took his pleasure from me was unlike anything I'd ever experienced. And the fact that he let me finish with him felt like a small miracle. As I lay there, content yet restless, I tried distracting myself with a book. But my attention kept slipping, pulled back to the heat and intensity of last night. Nothing in my past came close to what he gave me. And the thought that it might happen again sent a shiver of anticipation through me.

Eventually, I gave up on reading and decided a walk and some hot chocolate might clear my head. After slipping into my leggings, sweater, and Uggs, I check my phone. A text from my brother, sent late last night, catches my eye. He's canceled our morning coffee plans, saying he'd have to take a rain check. It worked out in the end.

Once I'm ready to go, I grab my things and open the front door. The cool morning air hits my face just as my foot hits something on the ground. Looking down, I freeze.

A wave of excitement surges through me, banishing all thoughts of hot chocolate and fresh air. There it is—that stupid little box with a red bow, sitting in my path like it has every time before.

I hate how much joy it brings me, the way butterflies erupt in my stomach at the sight of it. The thrill of wondering if he's watching me find it, the possibility that he's close by, sends a warm flush through me.

After last night, I know these gifts aren't just about my pleasure. They're about his control, his desire to command my body and my reactions. And yet... he knows exactly what I need. He knows how to ignite my senses, how to unravel me completely, how to take me apart and put me back together.

And now, staring down at the box, I know I'm caught in his web again. I can't help but wonder—what did he leave for me this time?

With trembling hands, I bend down and pick it up, untying the bow and opening the lid. The note is laying on top as always, and I unfold it, my heart racing.

'I will lay claim to every part of you. This is to ensure you enjoy it.'

I move the note aside, revealing what's nestled beneath it. My eyes widen as I stare down at the contents.

Three anal plugs, each a different size, are laying inside. The smallest has a white gem at the base, the medium-sized one green, and the largest—*massive*—is adorned with a red gem.

My breath catches as I pull them out one by one. The largest is... intimidating. Bigger than anything I own, bigger than I ever thought I'd even consider. And he expects me to use this? To put it *there*?

Heat floods my cheeks, and I quickly shove them back into the box, slamming the lid shut. No way. *Absolutely not.* I stuff the box into the drawer by my bed, as if hiding it could erase the image from my mind.

But I can't stop thinking about it.

Frustrated, I call Amara and ask if she can help me decorate. I need a distraction—something to pull me out of this spiral.

When she arrives, we spend the day together drinking eggnog and listening to Christmas music. The house finally starts to feel festive.

"Thanks for helping, Mar," I say, tucking my knees under me as we settle on the couch, admiring the tree.

She waves it off with a smile. "No big deal. You know I'll jump at any excuse to escape my mom's endless holiday plans. She has more Christmas spirit than a whole army of elves!"

I laugh, picturing her over-the-top decorations. "So, to get away from all that Christmas, you come help me decorate?"

Amara rolls her eyes, but she grins. "True, but at least you have taste."

She isn't wrong. I prefer simple elegance—white lights on the tree, a silver leaf garland, pearl ornaments, and a shining silver star on top. The rest of the house follows suit. The little Christmas village is set up, stockings are hanging from the mantle, and my snow globe collection is gleaming in its usual place.

When we finish, I feel a rare sense of peace settle over me. For the first time in a long while, I am not stuck in the past or weighed down by hurt and betrayal. Decorating wasn't just a distraction—it was for *me*.

I take a deep breath, letting the contentment sink in. For the first time in what felt like forever, I let myself feel joy.

We put on a Christmas movie from Netflix—one of those romantic comedies about a knight sent to the future who falls in love with a local woman who just got out of a bad relationship. She's trying to rebuild her life after being cheated on, and as much as I try to focus on the movie, I can't help but wish I could find love this year too.

When I was with Jake, I wasn't looking for anything long-term. But now, as I watch the couple on-screen find their happily-ever-after, I realize that I do want that kind of love. The forever kind. Just not with him.

About halfway through the movie, the guys come in, crowding the small living room. They decide to order pizza and join us. It's not unusual for us to all squish together on the couch—Amara and I usually claim the side with the chaise. But this time, with my brother sprawled there, she nudges me toward Damien instead. She rests her head on my brother's shoulder, and I make a mental note to talk to her about that later.

But right now, my mind is consumed by the man to my right.

Damien's thigh keeps brushing against mine, and I'm hyper-aware of every movement. His arm is draped casually over the back of the couch, but his fingers are lightly tracing circles on my shoulder. The gentle pressure sends a shudder through me, and I know he feels it. He leans in, inching closer, and I can feel the heat radiating off him.

This isn't unusual. We've sat like this plenty of times before, usually during scary movies, when I'd cling to him out of fear. But this isn't a scary movie. This is different.

My breath catches when his warm breath brushes the shell of my ear. His voice is low and teasing, "Why don't you relax, brat?"

I swallow hard, my pulse racing. Why does he have to get under my skin so easily?

I try to remind myself of all the reasons I shouldn't feel this way. He's my brother's best friend, for one. And I know if I ask him about this tension—this pull between us—I'll get burned. I'm not ready to risk being hurt again. I can't go through that.

But God, I'm drawn to him.

He's like an inferno, and I'm the foolish moth desperate to dive into the flames. The danger of it thrills me, but the fear of what might happen holds me back. I can't let myself fall, not when the stakes are this high.

Still, when he pulls me closer, I let him.

I relax against his side, his arm pulling me tighter, and for just a moment, I let myself imagine what it would be like if things could be different. If this tension didn't have to go unspoken. If I could let myself burn, just once, and feel the heat of him fully.

But for now, I stay quiet. Safe. And I let myself pretend.

Him

Every time I think about the gift, I left for her in the quiet, dark hours of the morning, I get hard. It's impossible to focus today. Every task I've tried to tackle has fallen by the wayside, my thoughts consumed by her—what I've done to her, what I *will* do to her, and how she responds so perfectly to every move I make.

Christmas Eve is coming fast, and I still have so much to prepare for her. She's been so good so far, letting me play my game, falling into every trap I've set. But the next few nights? They'll push her further than she's ever gone. If she can take it—and I know she will—she'll be rewarded.

I know she thinks I'll come to her tonight. And she's right. I will. But she won't see me. Not yet.

For now, I want to see how much she's come to expect me. How much she's starting to crave me. The absence will teach me as much as her presence. I won't touch her for the next few nights. I want to know how far she's willing to go, how much she can take, and what it feels like for her to miss me.

This isn't just about breaking her. It's about understanding her-knowing every boundary, every limit, and every desire she hasn't even discovered yet. Because when I finally reveal myself, when I finally claim her, I want there to be no question in her mind that I'm everything she needs.

I'll be the one to make her shatter. The one to make her whole.

And most importantly, she'll be *mine*.

Her

I wake up to the feeling of being shaken, jerking awake with a start.

"I didn't mean to scare you," Amara says, her face pink with embarrassment. "But you and Damien fell asleep together. Well, we all fell asleep."

I blink a few times, yawning as I stretch. The motion makes me acutely aware of the hard muscles wrapped around me, pulling me tighter as I move.

"Oh. What time is it?" I murmur groggily.

Amara checks her phone. "Just after six in the morning. I wanted to wake you up to say goodbye. I want to leave before everyone else wakes up." She glances at my brother, who's still sprawled on the couch.

We stayed up late, past one in the morning, watching movies. Sure, we got up for snacks, but we all returned to the same spots on the couch. And somehow, that spot ended up with me in Damien's arms.

Carefully, I wiggle free from his tightening grip. "Oh no, you don't," I whisper-yell at her. Slipping out completely, I point to Amara. "My room. Now," I demand in a hushed tone.

To her credit, she smiles mischievously and slips off to my bedroom. Once inside, with the door shut securely behind us, I turn to her. "Spill."

Amara hesitates, chewing nervously on her bottom lip. Something's definitely up, but I stay quiet, waiting her out. Finally, she groans and flops dramatically onto my bed.

"I don't know, Ana!" she exclaims, throwing an arm over her eyes. "One day, he's just my best friend's annoying big brother. The next, he's this... man who makes me question everything."

I perch on the bed beside her, studying her face. She's vulnerable in a way that catches me off guard.

"What's stopping you from going for it?" I ask softly. "You know how I feel about Damien, and how Jax feels about me being around his friends. It's hard, but I'd never want that for you. If you think he'll make you happy, go for it."

Amara sighs deeply and looks at me, her vulnerability turning into something resolute. "Because right now, it's nothing more than a crush," she says firmly. "You know how I am. I go through phases. And I know it's partly because of my breakup."

She's right. I understand all too well. My feelings for Damien, though, have never wavered.

I lean down and hug her. "You're sure?" I press gently.

She hesitates for a moment, then nods. "I'm sure," she says with conviction. She sits up and brushes her hands over her jeans. "I need to go home and pack for tomorrow. I'll see you later, okay?"

We exchange goodbyes, and she's gone. But even as I watch her leave, I can't ignore the ache in my chest. My mystery man didn't show. Again.

Needing caffeine to shake the lingering thoughts, I head to the kitchen. The familiar scent of coffee fills the air as I retrieve my phone from where I'd left it charging on the counter. No new messages.

The smell of the brewing coffee calms me, and I inhale deeply, letting the warmth settle my nerves. But when I open my eyes, they catch on something: a brown box with a bright red bow sitting on the counter.

I freeze.

I should feel violated. He came into my house while I was asleep—worse, while I was sleeping on another man. My stomach twists nervously. I know how possessive he can be. I've seen it. I've felt it. And while I may be a brat who pushes back, I'm not stupid.

Before I can second-guess myself, my feet move toward the box. Butterflies churn wildly in my stomach, a mix of nerves and excitement.

I position myself on the side of the island, keeping an eye on the living room in case anyone wakes up. The last thing I need is for them to see what's inside.

With one last glance at the couch, I pull the box toward me. It's rectangular, the size of a jewelry box, but I know it's not that. My fingers tremble as I tug at the ribbon, letting it fall away.

Inside is a note.

'I have wanted you for a long time, and when I finally get you, I don't plan on being gentle. I need you ready for me so you can enjoy it as much as I know I will. I don't want anything else getting that pussy ready for me but me. I will be seeing you soon, little angel.'

Beneath the handwritten note, another line is scrawled hastily in ink:

'P.S. You're lucky it was your brother's best friend you were sleeping on, or I'd get jealous.'

My heart races as I carefully remove the lid and pull out a velvet drawstring bag. The faintest sound from the living room snaps me out of my trance, reminding me that someone could walk in at any moment.

Gathering everything—the box, the bow, and my untouched coffee—I retreat to the safety of my room.

Once behind closed doors, I set everything on my dresser except the velvet bag. Sitting on the edge of my bed, I loosen the strings and dump the contents into my hand. If it weren't for the sheer size of the thing, I might've laughed.

In my palm is a candy cane-striped replica of my mystery man's dick.

Wrapping my fingers around it, I notice how they barely overlap. The damn thing has to be at least ten inches long. Suddenly, his note makes perfect sense. He'd said, *"You got me on Christmas Eve."* And judging by this, there's no way I could take him comfortably without some... practice.

A flush spreads through me as I imagine his intentions. He's going to use every hole I offer him—and the thought sends heat pooling between my thighs. The weight of the dildo in my hand suddenly feels heavier, almost demanding.

Before I can second-guess myself, I've stripped off my leggings and tossed them aside. Lying back on the bed with my legs spread, I let my fingers trail down, warming myself up. Just as I begin to lose myself in the moment, my phone beeps.

If it weren't for the custom tone I'd set for my mystery man, I would've ignored it.

> I take it you got my gift.

Frustrated, I quickly type out a response.

> I'm busy. What do you want?

His reply comes almost instantly.

> Don't you dare use my dick to get off. I want to watch as I stretch your tight little pussy for the first time.

His words only make me want to disobey. I grip the dildo and press the tip to my clit, teasing myself as I angle my phone for a better shot and hit record. Slowly, I slide the tip inside, just enough to stretch me, and let out a soft moan. I stop recording, then hit send, waiting for his reaction.

The typing bubbles appear, then disappear. They pop up again, linger, and vanish. This goes on for almost a minute before the screen flashes with an incoming video call.

I hit ignore, knowing he'll call right back. He doesn't disappoint.

This time, I answer the call—well, I click the button, but only a breathy moan escapes me.

He groans in response, "Fuck, little angel. If you know what's good for you, you'll stop."

At this point, I'm just messing with him. I put the toy down, not quite ready for it yet. Not without some serious preparation and practice. "Or you'll what? Come stop me?" I let my middle finger lazily stroke my clit, breathless, before pinching it, making me gasp and release a deep moan.

A low chuckle rumbles in my ears, the sound trailing down my spine and nestling in my core. "Oh, so you want to play games?"

With an exasperated sigh, I reply, "No, I want to cum."

I hear the smile in his words as he teases me next. "And you will… if you can listen."

"I think we've established that's not my strong suit," I breathe.

His laugh is low, almost as low as his words, keeping his voice a secret from me. "Ah, so you need some motivation." It's not a question. He knows me too well, he doesn't need confirmation.

I hum in response, moving my fingers slowly, teasing myself the way I imagine he would.

"You have two choices," he says, pausing long enough that I know he's waiting for me to pay attention.

I make him wait a beat before replying, "I'm listening."

"Good. One: You listen, and you get off to the sounds of me beating your ex for touching you."

My breath hitches, betraying my excitement. "And my second option?" I ask, sinking two fingers inside my slick folds.

His breathing grows heavy, and that thought turns me on even more. I did that to him—my voice, my body, my arousal.

"Or two: The next sounds you cum to will be the sounds of that pretty boy you were all cozy with tonight."

I freeze. Damien is innocent—he didn't touch me like Jake did. My stalker knows me too well; he knows I wouldn't want anything to happen to Damien.

But I cannot simply give in, I won't allow myself to show any weakness. Regardless of the fact he seems to already know my responses too well.

"That's a tough choice. But I think you could do better than last time," I murmur, emphasizing my point.

He practically growls his next words, "Don't push me. Be a good girl, grab the toy, and turn it on."

With a dramatic sigh, I reluctantly move to obey. "Done," I reply, my voice flat.

He only laughs in response, dripping with confidence as he says, "Now spread those pretty fucking thighs and slide it in. Nice and slow, feel it as it slides into your dripping cunt. I know you're wet for me, don't try to deny it."

His words manage to spur me on, no matter how much I hate myself for it. I need to save face. "You don't make me that wet," I protest weakly.

His low, smoky chuckle has me whimpering. "I will answer soon enough. Now, with the toy in, I want you to tell me a fantasy. One you want to act out with me."

My mind goes blank; I've thought of so many with him, I can't choose just one.

The vibrations start. "Is this from the other night?" I moan. His answering hum tells me everything I need to know. So does the unmistakable sound of his flesh hitting flesh.

I'm too lost in the haze of my pleasure and the mental image of my mystery man's possessiveness in action. My mouth opens involuntarily, words flowing freely from my lips.

"I want you to come to me when I'm asleep, like you did when you bound me."

The vibrations increase, and this time, knowing where they're from, drives the dark and depraved side of me closer to release.

Moaning, I continue, "Only this time, you would have slipped me something to make me sleepy, so I only wake for bits and pieces. But you'd know the truth, based on my body's reaction to you. I *want* it."

My breathing picks up, the mental picture is almost too much for me. His breathing grows faster, clearly just affected by this as I am.

"Fuck, such a good fucking girl," he growls, and I involuntarily clench. "Don't stop."

I'm not sure if he is talking about my words, or the feel of his fist gripping his cock, wishing it was my hand wrapped around him.

Maybe even a combination of the two. That thought drives me wild, but I manage to find my voice again.

My hands trails up to my breasts, pinching and tweaking my hardened nipples, sending zaps of electricity through my body. The intense sensation is heightened by the vibrations pulsing through my pussy, pushing me closer to the edge.

I force myself to get back to the matter at hand. "Then you would do whatever you wanted to me." I hesitate, but only for a second. "You would use me, use any hole you wanted and take your pleasure from me, leaving me shattered, used, and filled."

It's all too much, too intense. I can feel myself getting closer, I only need a little more.

A resounding moan follows my words, the sound guttural and raw. "You would let me do that to you?" he asks, desperate, and his strokes grow rapid—almost needy—as he speaks.

"You would let me take what I need from you, shatter your body, and trust that I would put you back together?" The emphasis on *need* isn't lost on me. "Before you answer, know this, little angel. Once I have you, I will not stop. I *will* leave my mark upon you. And I *will* use your body."

I don't doubt his words. Knowing him, it's a guaranteed fact and I'm counting on it.

"I know. I need you," I whimper, the impending orgasm building with an intensity and speed that threatens to pull me under.

He moans, an animalistic roar-like sound that makes me gasp. "You would let me have my way with you?" he asks again, as if he needs the confirmation. As if he doesn't already *know* it.

The sound that leaves my throat is one akin to a cry, pleasure taking over my body as I scream behind my arm, trying to muffle the sound. "Yes!"

Grunting is the only thing spilling over from the other line for a moment, my mystery man presumably too lost in his pleasure to respond.

"Fuck yes, my fucking little slut," he groans once he finds his voice again. "Just like that, choke that fucking dick."

His words fuel me, pushing me further over the edge. My pleasure crests like a wave, washing over me until I'm drowning, vanishing beneath the weight of the vibrations and his voice. I can't handle it, the pressure pulling me under and threatening to never let me up for air.

And for a moment, I wish I never will.

Him

Still breathing hard, I come down from the high. If she has me like this already, and I haven't even touched her yet... I can't imagine what it'll be like when I finally get my hands on her. Only five more days. Five. But I know I can't wait that long. I've made up my mind—I won't reveal myself to her until Christmas Eve. Until then, I'll have my fun.

Her heavy breathing comes through the other end of the call, each gasp winding tighter around my control.

"Fuck, little angel. The things I'm going to do to you," I say, my voice low and rough.

She whimpers, and the sound sends a sharp jolt straight to my dick. She can try to deny how I make her feel, but I know the truth. Her body betrays her—even over the phone.

Her voice, husky and laced with lust, shoots back, "Promises, promises."

She always makes me laugh, and tonight is no different. But I keep my voice low, careful not to give her any clues, not to let her figure me out too soon. She can't ruin the surprise—not yet.

With a smirk, I reply, "Get yourself cleaned up. I'll be seeing you soon."

Before she can say anything else, I end the call.

I exhale, my heart still pounding as I set the phone down. I need to get myself together. There's more shopping to do—and I have to make sure everything is perfect for Christmas Eve.

Her

Laughter fills the car as Amara and I head to the ski lodge. "There is no way!" I manage between gasps.

"I'm telling you, the guy was nuts!" she says, catching her breath. "He wanted to make out to Christmas music. In July, Anastasia! July!"

My sides ache as I laugh harder. "I can almost buy him asking you to dress up as the Virgin Mary, but inviting his two best friends to dress as the Three Wise Men? To make a 'new Christmas miracle'? Come on!" I wheeze, tears pooling in my eyes.

Every time either of us hears Silent Night, we think of this story, and it always leaves us in stitches. And honestly, I needed this today.

After my call with the mystery man yesterday morning, I pretty much passed out right where I was. Later, I double-checked my packing, got my toiletries ready, and spent the rest of the day reading a Christmas novella—a cute, fluffy story about a baker falling for the fire chief. It was such a refreshing change from the dark romances I'd been devouring lately—a nice palate cleanser.

The laughter finally dies down as the song ends. Amara wipes her eyes. "I sure dodged a bullet with that one," she says with a grin.

We've been on the road for two hours now, so we should be arriving soon. But my thoughts wander back to the brown box with the red bow. Before we left, I'd searched everywhere for it—but found nothing. I've been trying to ignore the disappointment that's been gnawing at me, but of course, Amara notices.

"What's going on?" she asks, shooting me a quick glance before turning back to the road.

I sigh, already knowing I won't fool her. "Nothing," I say weakly, though even *I* don't believe myself.

Amara isn't one to push. She knows I'll talk when I'm ready. But keeping this secret to myself is both fun and exhausting, so I decide to give her a little something.

"Fine," I admit. "I've sort of been talking to someone."

She squeals. "Please tell me it's Damien! I've seen the way you two look at each other."

I blush slightly. "No, not him." I glance out the window, trying to collect my thoughts. "Though... things between us have been getting heated. I really need to put a stop to it."

I don't have to look at her to know she's rolling her eyes. And she doesn't need me to explain why—it's a conversation we've had before. She falls silent, giving me space for the rest of the drive, knowing my mind is elsewhere.

When we finally arrive at the lodge, Amara excuses herself to the bathroom while I head to the check-in counter.

The concierge greets me with a friendly smile. He's cute—shaggy blonde hair, green eyes, and a warm demeanor. His name tag reads Nick. He's handsome in a way, though completely opposite from the dark brown eyes I crave. As I take him in, I notice the subtle sparkle of his piercings: two small studs in his ears and a tiny one in his nose. They catch the light just enough to draw my attention.

I must've stared a little too long because he grins flirtatiously as he checks me in. I don't miss the way he writes his number on the corner of my room information, his green eyes lingering on mine.

Before I turn to leave, he stops me. "Oh, and this was left for you," he says, pulling out a small brown box with a red bow.

My breath catches. I don't reach for it right away, my mind racing.

Amara's voice pulls me from my daze. Without thinking, I grab the box, still unsure what to feel—or how to explain it to her.

I waited all day to open the box. Just as I finally had it in my hands, Amara emerged from the bathroom. Not ready to explain anything yet, I quickly hid it. Later, once we got to our room and put our things down, we called the spa to check for availability. Luckily, they had one opening for a massage and one for a facial. It wasn't even a debate—I hate facials. We booked the appointments and hurried down.

Now that we're back, relaxed, and unwound, Amara has fallen asleep before the mix-and-mingle tonight. Taking advantage of the quiet moment, I pull out the box. I've been thinking about it all day. The biggest question gnawing at me is: How did he know I'd be here?

It takes me longer than I'd like to admit, but then I remember. I had posted something about this trip the night Jake showed up. Amara and I had taken pictures, all dressed up, and I captioned one: *Elk Ski Lodge, here we come!* Amara even commented on the event we were attending. All the information was right there for anyone to find.

Still feeling just as lost about my mystery man's identity as I could be, I finally open the box. I hesitantly start with the folded note inside.

'On the eighth night of Christmas, may your wildest dreams come true.'

I set the note aside and look at the item nestled in the box. A small pill. My heart skips as I immediately recognize it—it's tied to the fantasy I once described. The fact that he remembered, didn't question me, and didn't make me feel crazy for wanting this warms my chest in a way I can't ignore.

I know I shouldn't let my feelings grow for a stalker, but he's the only person who seems to see all of me and actually encourages me to embrace it.

While I'm still stuck staring at the pill, my phone buzzes with a text.

I take it you got your gift. Just know that if you want your fantasy to come true, all you have to do is take the pill tonight, and I'll take care of the rest. Enjoy your evening. I'll see you later, little angel.

I don't reply. There's no need. We both know what I'm going to do. I also know he's somewhere nearby, watching me.

With that thrilling thought lingering, I start unpacking some of my things. Thankfully, the cabin my parents chose is a cozy two-bedroom space with warm wood tones and red-and-cream accents. A real tree stands in the living room, decorated with colored lights, red and white bulbs, and an angel perched on top. The scent of pine fills the air, mingling with the comforting warmth of the fire crackling in the hearth. It's the perfect setting—I can already imagine curling up later in the oversized armchair with a good book.

Thankfully, the cabin has a small dresser and closet, perfect for organizing my belongings and hanging up the dress I plan to wear tomorrow night.

With that finished, I decide it's time to get ready for dinner. Tonight feels like a casual, cozy night. I turn to the bed, where I lay out three sweaters to decide what to wear tonight: a dark red long-sleeve shirt paired with a black vest, a loose-fitting cream cable-knit sweater, or a fitted light pink sweater with a cowl collar.

After some deliberation, I settle on the cream sweater. I pair it with dark brown leggings and the matching Uggs I got for Amara and myself. I sweep my hair into a loose, messy bun, letting a few strands frame my face, and go for a soft, no-makeup look. But just for fun, I add a bold wine-red lipstick. After a final glance in the mirror, I'm happy with what I see.

As I step out of the bedroom, Amara emerges from the one across the hall. She's wearing a dark red, long-sleeved sweater dress with tights and her own pair of matching Uggs.

"You look hot," I tell her with a grin. "But won't you get cold in tights?"

She smiles and flips her wavy brown hair over one shoulder. "Nope, they're fleece-lined."

I laugh, remembering how I got those for her last year. She had seen an ad online and wouldn't stop talking about them until I surprised her with a pair.

"Glad you still like them," I say. "Ready?"

She nods, and we both head toward the living room to grab our bags and my phone, which has been charging. Once we're ready, we step outside and begin the short, five-minute walk to the main building where the restaurant is located.

The crisp air fills our lungs as we walk, chatting about how excited we are for tomorrow's event. Well, mostly she talks—about the event, about the decorations, and about checking out the guys who pass by.

When we step inside the main building, I immediately notice the guy who checked us in earlier. He's standing with a group of men, all of them wearing matching dark green polos and tan khakis. It's clear this is the employee uniform. As we pass, all three smile at us, but the blonde one takes it a step further and waves.

Leaning in, Amara whispers, "Looks like that one has his eye on you," and then waves back.

I just smile. "Not my type," I reply casually. Because he's not.

Apparently, *my* type is a man I've probably never met—a man who can make my skin heat just by beating another guy for touching me, who sneaks into my room, ties me up, and uses one of my toys to drive me wild. *This* guy? He just looks... vanilla.

We make our way into the restaurant, which is bustling with people. While we wait for a table to open up, we head to the bar to grab drinks. It takes about fifteen minutes before we're seated, but the entire time, I feel the ghostly caress of eyes on me—eyes that I can only assume belong to my mystery man.

I try to search for him, glancing around casually, but it's pointless. The room is filled with dimly lit corners and darkened spaces where he could be lurking. Occasionally, I catch the blonde guy's gaze instead. Each time, I force myself to look away, unwilling to encourage him.

Every time I feel eyes on me, my chest tightens with anticipation. I scan the room, hoping for even the briefest glimpse of him, only to be disappointed. It's not him. It's never him.

"Girl, that guy keeps looking at you. You should go talk to him," Amara tries again, her persistence unwavering.

Sighing, I reply, "I told you, he's not my type."

She doesn't buy it this time.

Pausing, she holds her fork halfway to her mouth, a bit of Asian pear and walnut salad perched on it. "Bullshit. He is one hundred percent your type."

She's not wrong—or at least she wouldn't have been a few weeks ago.

"What's going on with you?" she asks, tilting her head in concern.

I set my fork down and take a moment to think about how to answer. Finally, I say, "It's not what I'm looking for anymore. After the Jake fiasco, I realized I want more. I want a meaningful relationship—something real, something I know or at least hope will go somewhere. I don't want a weekend fling."

Her smile tells me she understands. We finish dinner mostly in silence, though Amara keeps eye-flirting with a guy sitting at a table behind me. Meanwhile, I'm lost in thought, distracted by the constant feeling of eyes on me, searching for a gaze I can never seem to catch.

When the bill comes, we split it, and just as we're finishing, the guy Amara's been flirting with makes his way over to our table.

Sensing where this is headed, I give them some privacy and check my phone. A new message waits for me.

> I can't take my eyes off your mouth.

> I want your lips wrapped around my dick, leaving your mark.

A deep, dark, possessive part of me stirs at the thought. He wants me to mark him just as much as he wants to mark me.

Knowing his eyes are still on me, I smile to myself, scan the room one last time, then tuck my phone away.

Turning back to Amara, I catch the end of her conversation. The guy is asking if she'd like to go for an after-dinner walk. She glances at me, silently asking for permission the way best friends do.

Feigning a yawn, I say, "You go ahead. I think I'm going to head back to the room and get ready for bed early."

Her face lights up with excitement. "Are you sure you're okay?"

I nod. "Go, have fun. I'll see you later."

With that, she's up and out the door, following him.

I make my way back to the cabin, planning to change into something comfortable and read by the fire before settling in for the night. But as I walk, a small, secret smile creeps across my face at the thought of what's to come tonight.

His

This fucking brat. She knows exactly how to get under my fucking skin.

The way she read my message, scanned the room, and chose not to respond tells me everything I need to know; she wants to play out her little fantasy.

Throughout dinner, I stayed hidden. I could see her, but she couldn't see me. I also saw that little fucker who kept staring at her all night. Thankfully, she was too busy searching for me to pay much attention to him. Lucky for him—if she had, I would have had to do something about that.

When she finally gets up to leave, I know she's heading back to the cabin. Her best friend slips out another door with some guy, which I make a mental note to check on later. I need to make sure she's safe, too. But for now, my focus is entirely on the blonde beauty walking out toward the cabins.

I give her a head start, letting her get halfway to her cabin without noticing me. Still, based on her restless gaze at dinner, I know she's hyper-aware of my presence. It's like she *wants* to be caught.

Once I see her safely inside, I know I have an hour or two tops before I'll be needed back here. With time to spare, I decide to find her best friend.

It takes about forty-five minutes of searching before I spot her. She's stepping off a ski lift with the guy from dinner. His arm is casually draped over her shoulders, and she's just agreed to go back to his room.

Satisfied that she's safe, I make my way back to where my little angel should be waiting for me

By now, she's either already taken the sleeping pill or will be doing so shortly. Either way, it doesn't matter—I came prepared.

> I hope you're ready for me, little angel.

When I arrive at her cabin and see that she hasn't responded—or even read—my last text, I know she's asleep. The brat in her wouldn't have been able to resist a witty comeback otherwise.

Perfect.

Standing outside her cabin, I test the door and find she left it unlocked for me.

Stepping inside, I notice the only lights on are the ones on the tree and the warm glow of the roaring fire in the living room. The space feels quiet, intimate, and welcoming—just like her.

I make my way down the hallway, finding two doors. One is open, so I peek inside, but it's an empty room. That means she has to be behind the other door. Slowly, I turn to the door at my back. It's slightly ajar, and the room beyond is dark.

Before stepping in, I turn on the adjoining bathroom light, letting its faint glow spill into the bedroom. I remain as quiet as possible, careful not to wake her.

Once inside, I head straight for the bench under the window. Reaching behind it, I grab what I stashed there earlier.

The first item is a mask—carefully chosen for tonight. It covers most of my face, leaving only my mouth and chin exposed. The short black feathers covering it give the illusion of slicked-back hair, while the horns sprouting from the temples add a monstrous touch. They curve out and back, almost meeting in the middle with just two inches of space between them. The smooth, weathered texture of the horns mimics the bark of an ancient tree.

Around the eye openings, the feathers lighten, shifting to dark brown with an almost white strip bordering the inner edge. Chocolate-brown centers dot the lighter feathers, while black lace frames the eyes, adding a final touch of elegance. I know she loves monster books, and I chose this mask specifically to make her fantasies feel real.

After adjusting the mask into place, I grab the other item I'd prepared. I may have snuck into her room earlier to get it, but I know she'll thank me for it later. I only have a few days to make sure she's ready for me, and I intend to make every moment count.

With everything set, I approach the bed and take a moment to look at my little angel. She's lying on her back, one arm thrown above her head, her fingers resting on the pillow. Her hair, still slightly damp, spills loosely from a tie at the nape of her neck. Her other hand rests lightly on her stomach, atop the tan comforter.

Her face is bare, free of makeup—even the wine-red lipstick I told her I liked. She's wearing what looks to be a black tank top, though it might be a nightgown. I'll find out soon enough.

I allow myself a moment to take her in, committing every detail to memory. She's even more beautiful like this—unguarded, vulnerable, mine.

As I step closer to her, I notice the box I left at the check-in counter is open, and the contents are gone. Next to it is a glass of water. Between her not responding to my text and now this, it's all I need to know: she wants this.

Before I start, though, I need to fix something. I move to her bathroom, assuming that's where her makeup bag would be.

Once I find it, I dig through it and pull out what I'm searching for—her lipstick. I told her I wanted her lips to paint my cock, and they will.

Walking back into the bedroom, I see she hasn't moved at all. I'm hoping she'll wake up at some point; I only gave her a sleeping pill. It shouldn't knock her out completely.

Making my way back to her on the bed, I carefully apply more lipstick to her lush, beautiful lips. It's a little messy, but it will be worse once I'm done. With that reapplied, I move to pull the blanket down her body, revealing a black nightgown that falls to mid-thigh.

Before I move to the end of the bed, I pause at the edge and free myself, already hardening at the thought of smearing her lipstick. I slowly fist my cock, stroking myself as I look at her until I'm fully hard. Then I gently tilt her head so I can access her mouth properly.

Before easing myself into her mouth, I rub the tip of my swelling cock over her lips, smearing a bead of precum on them. Then, I press into her mouth, careful not to go too deep to avoid waking her. But as her lips envelop me, I'm willing to take the risk.

I don't want to fuck her face—not yet. When I do, she'll be awake and on her knees for me, looking up at me with those intoxicating eyes. Right now, I just want her lipstick marks on my cock. Slowly, I thrust in as deeply as she can take me. When I pull back, I see the marks from her lipstick, just as I wanted.

I want to remember this. I want her to see her mark on my skin, claiming me and reflecting the truth I already know—I'm hers. I pull out my phone, and angle it so the stain on my cock is visible, before snapping a picture—one with my dick still in her mouth, the red ring in perfect view. I'm surprised that jostling didn't wake her, but it's all the better for me.

With that done, I pull the rest of the way out of her mouth, and tuck myself back in my pants, moving to the end of the bed.

For a moment, I simply look at her. She's so relaxed, so innocent, so intoxicatingly beautiful. And her body is about to learn how it feels to be worshipped.

I kneel at the foot of the bed, and place my palms on her legs, trailing slowly up until her soft thighs are gripped in my hands, my hold hard enough to pull a whimper from her. She stirs slightly, but thankfully doesn't wake up, and I continue my perusal. I lightly place my knees between her legs, nudging them apart to create room for my body. With newfound access, I work her nightgown up to her hips, revealing her perfectly bare for me, her cunt right there for me to feast on.

The view is too much for me. I can't hold myself back, the need to taste her clouding my senses. I lean down, careful not to wake her, until I'm comfortably nestled between her legs, and kiss the soft skin of her inner thighs. From here, her scent is torture—a heady mix of what must be her trade rose-scented body wash.

I move my head up slowly, trailing kisses higher and higher, and with each kiss, my grip on her tightens, until I get to her center and stop. With some quick and light maneuvers, I move her legs so they're resting on my shoulders.

My hands, now free, move to her bare cunt, spreading her open so close to my mouth I can practically taste her already. And because the temptation is too much, I do, dragging the flat part of my tongue against her like she's my favorite flavor of ice cream, and I finally get the first real taste of my little angel. She moans, a tiny whisper of a breath, and I flick her clit in response, before sucking it lightly in my mouth. Her hips buck and grind against my face, and I resist the urge to grin—even in her sleep, she's so responsive to me.

Having her like this, spread out and writhing for me in her sleep, has my already hard dick straining to get free. My control was already hanging by a thread, and I knew that once I tasted her, it wouldn't be enough. I'm just addicted to her.

Her moans progressively grow in volume and intensity, her body responding to my touch more and more, and I know she's ready. I can taste it, her wetness flowing into my mouth, and a wave of satisfaction runs through my body in a shiver.

"That's it, little angel, get fucking wet for me," I whisper against her now-dripping cunt.

Now that she's ready, the *real* fun can begin.

I slide a gloved finger inside her, testing her tightness, gauging how much preparation she'll need for what I have planned. She's just as snug as I remembered—perhaps even more so. My little angel starts rocking against me, seeking more, needing more. I oblige her, slipping a second finger into her warmth and feeling her clench around them. I pause briefly, savoring the moment as I capture another picture of her.

Resuming with slow, deliberate thrusts, I work her open, my fingers exploring, coaxing, until I can press a third inside. Her soft whimpers turn into breathy moans, her body responding beautifully. Curling my fingers, I find her most sensitive spot, pressing and stroking until her moans grow louder, needier. She's ready.

Reaching for the near-perfect replica of my cock—a candy-cane-striped toy—I press it to her swollen clit, rubbing in slow circles as her body shivers with anticipation. I withdraw my fingers from her, their slickness coating my glove, and use her arousal to lubricate the toy. Aligning it with her entrance, I notch the tip at her opening, savoring the sight of her beginning to stretch for me.

I take my time, easing the toy in and out, each thrust a little deeper than the last. Her body quivers as she adjusts, the tight heat of her gripping the silicone. The sight is *intoxicating*. The toy is nearly buried inside her, but I won't push it further tonight. Only I will claim her fully—only I will brand her from the inside out.

Needing to immortalize this moment, I snap one final picture of her glistening cunt stretched tightly around the toy. Then, tossing my phone aside, I focus my full attention on the angel in front of me, ready to make her completely mine.

Her breathing quickens, her moans growing louder as her hips grind in a desperate rhythm. She's so close, and I know it. I lean forward, capturing her clit in my mouth, sucking hard enough to make her gasp.

Glancing up, I catch her gaze, those striking blue eyes that I can never get enough of. But instead of surrendering, she smirks through her pleasure. "Who are you supposed to be? Big Bird's demon brother or something?" she teases, her voice breathless but defiant.

I can't help the smile that tugs at my lips, pressing against her heat. "Bratty to the bitter fucking end, aren't you?" I murmur, my voice low and dark.

She rolls her eyes, and then her hips, challenging me. And just like that, my control snaps. I don't care that it's just a toy. I lean closer, my tone dangerous, possessive. "One day soon, I will fuck you so thoroughly, my mark will be inside you forever. No other man will even come close to making you feel like this. Only me."

I press my weight onto her, moving harder, pushing her limits. She winces briefly, but the moan that follows tells me she loves it, craves it.

Her eyes flutter, the fight to keep them open warring against the haze threatening to pull her under. She struggles, but eventually, they fall closed for a few moments.

The sight of her surrender ignites something primal in me. Rising to my knees, I reach out, grabbing her breast with one hand while the other moves to my zipper. The sound is almost deafening in the charged silence. I free my cock, hard and throbbing, stroking myself as I take her in.

She's perfect. And she's mine.

With one hand, I work the toy deeper and harder, each thrust coaxing more pleasure from her trembling body. My other hand wraps tightly around my aching cock, stroking in time with the rhythm I've set for her—fast, relentless, and consuming. Her moans fill the room, a symphony of need and surrender.

She stirs beneath me, her eyes fluttering open, catching me in the act of stroking myself over her. There's fire in her gaze, fevered and unashamed, as she watches me with raw hunger.

"I'm so close," she whines, her voice trembling with desperation.

And then it happens. Her body arches, her head falling back as a scream of pure pleasure tears from her throat. The sight of her unraveling, knowing she came around the toy I worked into her, pushes me over the edge. I groan deeply, my release spilling across her stomach, trailing up to her exposed breasts.

Her chest heaves, her breathing erratic, as she begins to come down from her high. But when I don't slow down, she tenses. "Stop. Please, I—please, I have to pee," she gasps, her voice laced with panic.

A knowing smile tugs at my lips, but I don't stop. "Just trust me," I murmur, trying to reassure her, my voice soft but firm.

She shakes her head frantically. "No, please stop! I really have to pee," she insists, her panic mounting.

For a moment, I hesitate. I know she's overwhelmed, her mind clouded by the lingering effects of the sleeping pills. I shouldn't push her—not like this. With a sigh, I pull the toy from her slowly, and she winces as it slides free.

The moment she's untethered, she scrambles out of bed and darts to the bathroom.

I use the opportunity to clean myself up and slip out quietly. I know her well—her stubbornness, her need to do things on her terms. Next time, she won't stop me. I'll take the time to explain everything, to show her there's nothing to fear. But for now, I'll let her process this moment in her own way.

Her

After my masked mystery man had his fun last night, I made him stop—something I regret now. I don't know what came over me; there was this overwhelming urge to pee, so I panicked and told him to stop. But when I got to the bathroom, nothing happened. No matter how hard I tried, I couldn't go.

I wanted to ask him about it, but it felt... weird. Plus, by the time I crawled back into bed, my head barely hit the pillow before I was out cold.

When I woke up this morning, just after nine, I felt groggy—no doubt from the sleeping pill I took. Not that I'm complaining. I also woke up deliciously sore, which doesn't surprise me at all. Sitting here now, over an hour later, curled up by the fire with my coffee and a book, I can't help but smirk at the dull ache in my body.

What did surprise me was the damn toy—his replica—lying on the bed next to me. It wasn't where I left it. It should have been tucked away in the bedside drawer... at home, a hundred miles from here.

I remember most of last night. Waking up with his head between my thighs, the mask hiding his face, giving me nothing to work with—no hints about who he is. If it hadn't been such a rush, I'd probably be freaking out.

My thoughts are interrupted when Amara walks through the door, pulling me from my book—not that I've been paying much attention to it anyway.

"Oh, I didn't realize you didn't come back last night," I tell her.

She raises an eyebrow, giving me a look like I've lost it. "I texted you last night to say I wasn't coming back. Then again twenty minutes ago to let you know I was on my way."

Heat floods my cheeks. "Oh, I didn't see them. When I got back last night, I read until I couldn't stay awake. Then I went to bed. I guess I forgot to plug my phone in." It's not entirely a lie—I did read until I couldn't stay awake. I just left out the part about why.

She shakes her head with a knowing smile. "Figures. Only you would come to a beautiful place like this, full of attractive men, and spend the night curled up with a book." She laughs lightly, teasing me.

Feigning offense, I clutch my chest dramatically. "I beg your pardon, but there is an entire community of readers who would happily choose a masked, fictional man—possessive and downright filthy—over some real-life creep who can't stop staring at a chest for more than two minutes."

She laughs harder, holding up her hands. "Fair enough." She moves past me toward the hallway. "I'm going to shower and then take a nap. See you later."

Before she disappears into her room, she calls back, "Enjoy your book, nerd."

I smile at her term of endearment. Amara has never been one for books; she's always preferred the real thing. Still, she lets me geek out over my current read, humoring me enough to pretend she's interested.

Her mention of texting me makes me curious about what else I might have missed. Setting my book down, I get up to find my phone. Once it's plugged in and has enough charge, I turn it on. Notifications immediately flood the screen.

Among the texts and missed calls, a few messages from my masked mystery man catch my eye, and my heart skips a beat.

> Maybe next time you'll trust me.

> I know what you needed, and it wasn't for me to stop.

> You were about to cum for me.

I'm not entirely sure he's right, but the fact that I couldn't go when I thought I needed to has me questioning things. I might have to ask Amara about it.

After sitting back down to read, a sudden wave of exhaustion washes over me. Deciding I could use the rest, I head to bed and quickly fall asleep.

When I wake up and roll over to check the time, it takes me a moment to realize I've been out for almost four hours. Unlike this morning, I feel alert, refreshed, and ready—perfect timing, considering the Christmas party starts in a couple of hours. Amara and I will need to start getting ready soon.

But first, I need to eat. Skipping breakfast this morning was clearly a mistake, and sleeping this long didn't help. Not wanting to ruin my appetite for dinner later, I settle on something small: a peanut butter and jelly sandwich. It's just enough to tide me over until dinner at seven, though I know there'll be hors d'oeuvres during the cocktail hour.

Sandwich in hand, I head to wake up Amara, but the sound of running water coming from her bathroom stops me. Poking my head in, I call out, "Hey, I'm going to shower too."

She calls back, "Okay! I just got in, so I'll be a bit."

Satisfied, I head to my room and start my own shower.

The moment I step under the hot water, I feel tension I didn't even realize I was carrying melt away. The heat soothes my sore muscles, though a small part of me relishes the dull ache. The soreness is a reminder of last night, and I can't help but smile. I know I won't have to wait much longer to have him—completely—but I'm willing to play his game. Letting the anticipation build feels like the right move. Something tells me it will be worth it.

Feeling more relaxed, I go through my usual shower routine. When my hair and body are clean, I turn off the water, step out, and wrap myself in a towel. One for my hair, one for my body.

I'm halfway to my bedroom when I stop short.

There, on my dresser, sits a brown box tied with a red bow.

I feel my heart skip as I let go of the towel around my body. The cool air brushes my skin, making my nipples peak, but I barely notice. My focus is locked on the box.

Crossing the room, I pick it up and open it.

Inside, there's a picture of his dick—nothing surprising there—but the picture itself catches me off guard. It's in my mouth. I didn't even realize he'd taken it. The thought makes my mouth water, and the note beneath the photo has my legs clenching.

'On the ninth night of Christmas, I let you mark me as yours. The mark left by your pretty red lips wrapped around my dick. It is yours, little angel. I am yours.'

I don't know why that satisfies something deep inside me, but it does.

"Hey! Have you decided on your hair yet?" Amara's voice breaks through my thoughts.

Snapping out of it, I quickly tuck the picture into the outer pocket of my bag before answering. "Yeah, I decided on wearing it down!"

Pulling myself together, I grab a black button-up shirt and a pair of loose-fitting gray shorts, slipping them on. I like wearing a button-up while getting ready—it's easy to take off without messing up my hair or makeup.

Since I have the bathroom with the double vanity, Amara joins me as we get ready. We tackle our hair first, which takes about an hour, then move on to makeup. Another hour later, we're both done and head back to our rooms to get dressed.

When it's time for the big reveal, we step into the hallway at the same time.

Amara looks stunning. Her burgundy dress is fitted, with a flowy tulle overlay that gives her every movement an ethereal quality. Her beachy waves cascade over her shoulders, and her subtle smokey eye makes her brown eyes pop. A sheer cherry-red gloss adds just enough color to her lips.

"You look amazing!" I gush as she gives a twirl.

She fans herself dramatically. "If only I were into women," she teases.

I laugh, but her compliment makes me stand a little taller. My emerald-green dress hugs my curves in all the right places. The long sleeves give it an elegant touch, while the exposed back and high slit up my thigh add a sexy edge. The scoop back dips almost to the curve of my ass, and the ruching under my left breast pulls everything in perfectly.

I can't remember the last time I felt this confident.

"Your turn," Amara says, grinning.

I give her a slow twirl, letting her take it all in.

"Damn," she says, pretending to fan herself. "You're going to turn heads tonight."

Feeling ready to take on the night, we grab our jackets and head out the door.

Him

I've been watching her all night.

The moment she stepped into the room, it was as if she were a vortex, commanding everyone's attention without even trying. She captivated the crowd effortlessly, her light shining brighter than anyone else's. She may be a brat, but she's also magnetic—like the North Star. Impossible to ignore, and once you find it, you can't look away.

Men circle her like moths to a flame, desperate for her attention. They remind me of stray dogs, hoping for scraps, and she indulges them just enough to keep them wagging their tails.

But something shifts when the man I entrusted with the box approaches her. There's a noticeable change in the air. The other men seem to back off as if sensing she's been spoken for. They linger on the periphery, watching, waiting to see what unfolds.

What I don't expect is for her to give him the time of day.

I feel the burn of jealousy flare up instantly, hot and all-consuming. My hand moves to my phone before I even think twice, and I send her a warning.

> If you know what's good for you—and that little fucker—you won't entertain his notion that he has a chance.

She pulls her phone from her bag, reads the message, and then scans the room. Her eyes dart from one corner to the next, searching for me. When she doesn't find me, she smirks, slips her phone away, and makes a show of taking his.

She leads him to a table, pulling him down into a chair beside her. He leans closer almost immediately, his body language oozing possessiveness as he slides even closer. My jaw clenches, and I fire off another message.

> You do not want to test me right now, little angel.

This time, when she retrieves her phone, she responds.

> Oh, I think I want to. Have a fun night.

Then she silences her phone, making a point of ensuring I see it, and turns her attention back to him.

For the rest of the event, I'm forced to watch from the shadows. Forced to endure the sight of her letting this idiot flirt with her while she entertains him, knowing it's driving me insane.

He drapes his arm casually over the back of her chair, his hand brushing her bare back whenever he gets the chance. I can see the subtle tension in her shoulders, the slight discomfort in her expression, but she tolerates it. She does it to rile me up, to push me closer to the edge.

The final straw comes when he leans in, whispering something into her ear, his fingers tracing a line up the slit of her dress.

That's when I see it—the way her body shifts away from him, the unease in her movement. It does little to temper the anger boiling inside me.

She will learn a lesson tonight.

Her

All night, I've felt his eyes on me. His gaze is like a touch, hot and heavy, and knowing he's watching is the only reason I've entertained this insufferable fuckboy.

Nick hasn't shut up about himself for the past hour. I couldn't tell you half of what he's said, but the smug grin on his face tells me he thinks he's killing it. He's not.

The second I stop feeling my mystery man's eyes on me, I take my chance to escape. I quickly locate Amara—still wrapped up with the same guy from last night—and let her know I'm heading back to the cabin.

Unfortunately for me, Nick follows.

He's been tagging along like an overeager puppy, but by the time we reach the cabin, he grows bolder. He moves closer, his confidence swelling, and leans in like he's about to kiss me.

I step back, putting space between us. "Sorry, Nick, but some, uh... girl things came up, and I need to take care of it."

It's a weak excuse, one I never use, but it's the fastest way to kill his enthusiasm.

His expression pales at the implication. "Oh! Uh, yeah, for sure. No problem. I'll, uh, head back and find my buddies. Catch you later."

He doesn't even spare me a second glance as he retreats quickly down the path.

Once I'm safely inside, I exhale, finally alone. Needing to unwind, I make myself a peppermint hot chocolate and curl up on the couch with my phone in hand. I hesitate, staring at the dark screen, nervous to turn it back on after everything I did tonight.

I know I pushed him too far. I can feel it.

When I finally press the power button, the phone takes a few moments to boot up. Deciding to put off the inevitable, I focus on getting ready for bed instead. My nightly routine drags on for at least five minutes—longer if you count the time it takes to brush my teeth, which I'm saving until after I finish my drink.

Once I'm settled under the covers, peppermint cocoa finished, I finally open my phone.

The notification bar lights up, but only one message matters:

> I hope you enjoyed your night. I know I will.

My stomach drops.

A shiver runs through me, my breath hitching as the words sink in. My pussy clenches, still tender from last night, and the thought of anything touching me there is both thrilling and terrifying. My body craves him, aches for him, even as my sore muscles protest the idea.

What does he mean?

The question circles my mind as I lie there, trying to piece together his cryptic message. My thoughts churn for what feels like hours, but exhaustion catches up to me, pulling me into a restless sleep.

***

I wake up with a jolt, a deep moan escaping before I can fully grasp my surroundings. My gaze drops instinctively, and there he is—my masked mystery man, his presence commanding as he kneels between my thighs. Before I can recover, a sharp sensation shoots through me as his hand connects with my clit with precision.

"If you want to act like a tease," he says, his voice low and edged with authority, "I'll treat you like one."

To emphasize his point, another swift slap leaves me gasping. I open my mouth to protest, but before any words can form, he moves, quick and deliberate. In mere moments, he's on his knees between my thighs again, leaning over me, one hand braced against the wall above.

His movements are purposeful, calculated, torturously grinding his hardened length against my stinging clit. As his body presses closer, I feel his presence in every nerve, every inch of space between us. When I try to speak again, he interrupts me with the replica of his cock in my mouth, silencing me completely. His intensity, both physical and emotional, leaves no room for objection.

"You like to run your mouth too much," he murmurs, his tone low and almost teasing as he leans in closer, "so I might as well put it to good use."

A quiet sound escapes me at his words—a mixture of frustration and something deeper I can't quite name. My moans seem to fuel him, and he pushes the toy until it reaches my throat—clearly trying to make me gag, but I refuse to give him that satisfaction. Instead, I relax, breathing slowly through my nose, my nails leaving crescent moons on my palms. At first the pain distracts me from the force, but I inevitably gag in the end.

"That's it, little angel," he mockingly praises. "Get it nice and wet for me."

I glare at him in response, and he tilts his head slightly, studying me as though trying to read my every thought, every response. My eyes drift to the feathered mask he wore, the soft edges of it contrasting with the dark, sharp horns that frame his head. His gaze meets mine, intense and unreadable, obscured further by the dim light that makes it impossible to discern the true color of his eyes.

He keeps fucking my face with the toy, tears streaming down my face, but suddenly, the details of his attire strike me—a fitted black button-down and slacks that give him a refined, almost polished air. He's dressed for the party. How did I miss him earlier?

As if sensing my thoughts, he shifts again, his expression softening ever so slightly. "Good girl," he said, his voice dripping with approval.

The words catch me off guard, resonating in a way I hadn't anticipated. Heat blooms across my skin, and I find myself caught between the desire to resist and the pull of his quiet praise. The world seems too narrow, his words grounding me even as they unraveled something deeper.

I've only ever read about the power of words like his, but now I feel it firsthand. His praise melts me, making me more willing, more pliant. I crave hearing it again, even if it means surrendering a little more of myself to him.

After another moment, he shifts, sliding back down my body, his gaze locked on mine. The toy in his hand leaves my mouth, tracing a deliberate path—down my chin, between my clothed breasts, across my stomach, and lower. My breath catches as the tip grazes my sensitive clit. Then, with unnerving precision, he strikes again, delivering another sharp slap that makes me cry out.

This time, though, he doesn't stop there. His mouth replaces the fleeting sting with something deeper, sweeter, and far more intoxicating. His tongue works with a practiced rhythm, drawing out pleasure and sounds I can't hold back. When he pauses to murmur, "You taste so sweet. I knew I'd be addicted from the first taste," the raw honesty in his voice sends a shiver down my spine.

I tip my head back, overwhelmed, my words tumbling out unbidden. "I'm close. Don't stop."

But just as quickly as the sensation builds, his tongue stops. My eyes snap open. "What the fuck?" I demand, glaring down at him.

He chuckles softly, his lips glistening as he replies, "As much as I'd love for you to cum on my tongue, I want to see you fall apart on my cock tonight." His words are a promise, sealed by the press of the toy as he slides it into my aching cunt with a deliberate, unyielding motion.

I barely have time to adjust before he pushes it deeper, setting a pace that's slow and exacting, each movement calculated to remind me who's in control. But it doesn't stay slow for long. His movements grow harder, more demanding as he brutally thrusts the toy in my pussy. It's almost too much—almost—but I find myself arching into it, meeting his rhythm with a hunger that surprises even me.

The pleasure builds quickly, a rising wave that threatens to pull me under. My breath hitches as incoherent sounds spill from my lips, my hips bucking to match his rhythm. But just when I feel myself teetering on the edge and my back arches off the bed, he stops again, pulling the toy away.

My frustration flares. "If you keep stopping, I'll finish it myself."

The growl that rumbles from his chest is low and warning as I move to grab the toy. In an instant, my wrists are pinned above my head, his grip firm but not painful. He leans closer, his breath warm against my ear as he thrusts the dildo back in my aching pussy, just as brutally as before. "I think you've tested me enough tonight, don't you?"

I meet his gaze with a smirk. "Not even close."

His smile is slow and deliberate. "I was hoping you'd say that."

This time, his movements leave no room for teasing. His fingers begin rubbing my clit, his pace relentless and each motion designed to pull me apart piece by piece. He's rubbing with a maddening precision, and I fight to hold on, clenching every muscle and willing myself not to give in. I refuse to show him how close I am.

The sound of the cabin door creaking open jolts me. "Are you up?" Amara's voice calls out, clear and close.

Before I can react, his gloved hand covers my mouth, muffling any sound. He leans down, his voice a low whisper in my ear. "Unless you want me to stop, stay quiet."

I glare up at him, torn between defiance and a need to protect my secret. Amara doesn't need to know—not yet. With a reluctant nod, I concede, and his smirk deepens.

Once again, he slides down my body, his mask still in place as his hands push my thighs further apart. The sight of him—focused, unrelenting as he eats me out and fucks me with the toy—is ridiculously sexy and almost too much. I have to look away, fearing that even meeting his eyes would betray me with the sounds I struggle to hold back.

When he sucks my clit back into his mouth, I barely hold it together. The sensation is overwhelming, teetering on the line between pleasure and pain. My resolve wavers as I open my mouth, releasing a silent scream into the air.

Sensing my unraveling, he slows just enough to pull me back from the brink, removing his mouth and slowing his thrusts of the dildo.

Frustration courses through me, and I slam my fists against the bed. "You can't make me cum," I taunt, the challenge clear in my voice.

His eyes darken at my words, the reaction exactly what I was hoping for. With renewed intensity, he sets to work, the toy fucking me in tandem with his mouth. Every motion, every flick of his tongue, pushes me further than before. He works me to the point it almost stings—my clit is clearly overstimulated. The sensations build and build, cresting in waves that leave me breathless and on the edge of something I can't escape.

I feel utterly used and desperate in ways I've never experienced before. At first, I revel in the intoxicating pleasure he forces from me, so unlike anything I've felt before. But his relentless game of hot and cold quickly vanishes my patience.

"If you're not going to let me finish, then get off me, and I'll do it myself," I snap, my frustration finally boiling over.

To my surprise, he moves. Settling back on his heels, he regards me with that infuriating smirk of his. The chuckle that follows grates against my already frayed nerves. "I'd like to see you try, little angel," he teases, his tone dripping with arrogance.

I glare at him, but he's already unzipping his pants, pulling his cock free with a deliberate slowness that makes my pulse quicken despite my anger. Ignoring him, I slide my hand down my body to my clit, fully expecting him to stop me, to take control the way he has all night.

But he doesn't move.

His lack of reaction both annoys and emboldens me. I start working my clit, circling and pressing with growing urgency, desperate to chase what he's so cruelly denied me. He matches my movements, stroking his cock in tandem, his pace quickening as I try to push myself over the edge.

But no matter how fast or hard I work, it isn't enough. My body betrays me, too overstimulated and raw to find release. A frustrated whine escapes my lips, unbidden, as I gasp, "Please. Just let me finish." My pride holds me back from outright begging, but the desperation in my tone is unmistakable.

His breath hitches, his pace faltering for just a moment before he groans and spills his hot cum across my pelvis. The heat of it spreads over my sensitive skin, making me gasp, though not in satisfaction. His words follow, low and commanding, as he tucks himself back into his slacks. "I control your pleasure now, little angel."

That's the last straw. Before he could stand, I shove him off the bed with all the strength I can muster and storm into the bathroom, slamming the door behind me. His laughter follows me, light but maddening. "I don't like to share," he calls out before the room falls silent.

I stay in the bathroom far longer than necessary, the hot water soothing my frayed nerves as I scrub away the lingering evidence of him. Even after I finish, I linger, trying to collect myself.

When I finally emerge, the room is quiet and empty. The first rays of dawn slip through the curtains, bathing everything in pale morning light. A glance at the clock confirms it was six in the morning. I didn't realize how much of the night had passed.

The bed is just as I'd left it, disheveled and empty—except for a small brown box tied with a neat red bow. My first instinct is to throw it away, anger still simmering beneath the surface. But curiosity gets the better of me.

Carefully, I open the box, pulling out a folded note on crisp paper. My stomach twists as I read the words:

'I already warned you about other men touching you. Perhaps this will help jog your memory.'

A cold chill runs down my spine as I set the note aside and peer into the box's contents. What I see makes my blood drain from my face. Nestled inside are three pieces of jewelry—each stained with dried blood.

Him

I originally planned to drug her and toy with her again tonight, but after her little performance, I decided against it. She needed to be fully aware for this lesson to sink in.

It took everything in me not to storm across the room and rip his hand off her thigh. The rage I felt was barely contained, and once she was gone, I made sure he learned what it meant to touch what was mine. He's lucky I stopped at ripping out his earrings and that ridiculous nose ring. The desire to strip away every inch of skin that had made contact with her burned in me, but I knew my little angel wouldn't appreciate such a gift.

As I walk back to my room, my thoughts shift to the end game. Just one more night. One more night to play with her, to watch her squirm, before I reveal myself fully. By Christmas morning, she *will* be mine in every sense—body, mind, and soul.

The thought of finally sinking into her, feeling every inch of that tight, wet warmth wrapped around me, sends a shiver of anticipation down my spine. I won't hold back. The need to claim her completely, to cum deep inside her and make her mine in the most permanent way, consumes me.

The idea of her glowing, carrying my child, fills me with a primal hunger I can barely contain. She will be mine, and nothing—not her defiance, nor anyone else—will stand in my way.

Taking in the sharp morning air, I quicken my pace. I still have things to take care of before that idiot tries to turn me in.

Her

Since Amara drove us back from the lodge, she dropped me off on her way home. She had to get to her grandparents' house for the annual Christmas Eve Eve dinner with her dad's side of the family. Tomorrow, she'd head to her mother's side for their Christmas Eve dinner. Then, it'd just be her, her parents, her older brother, and his new wife at their house on Christmas Day. Amara always complained about the whirlwind of holiday obligations, but without fail, she came back with the best stories to share when she joined me after my family's dinner.

We said our goodbyes in the car since she was cutting it close, and I waved as she drove off.

Once inside, I make a beeline for the kitchen. We left the lodge early to beat traffic and so Amara could help her grandmother cook. With nearly her entire extended family coming over, they always started preparations early.

With a fresh cup of coffee in hand, I lean against the kitchen island, admiring my Christmas tree. The scent of cinnamon, honey, and vanilla mingle from the coffee grounds and frosted gingerbread creamer, creating a moment that feels like Christmas itself. I close my eyes, letting the warmth of the mug seep into my palms, and take a slow, deep sip. The rich flavors wrap around my soul like a comforting blanket.

When I open my eyes, something under the tree catches my attention.

A box.

This one is larger than the others and wrapped in the same brown paper with a red bow, immediately signaling who it's from. My heart skips a beat.

I know I have to get it out of sight before anyone comes home. Moving faster than I care to admit, I rush to the tree, grab the box, and hurry up to my room.

Settling onto my bed, I untie the bow with shaky fingers and read the note tucked on top.

'No more games, little angel. Tomorrow I will claim you.'

The words send a shiver down my spine. Setting the note aside, I tear through the wrapping paper to reveal a plain box. My thighs press together involuntarily as I lift the lid.

Inside are smaller boxes, each neatly wrapped and numbered. I realize belatedly they're meant to be opened in order, but curiosity gets the better of me. With a shrug, I rip them all open and lay the contents out in front of me.

The largest box holds a leg spreader—long, sleek, and adorned with padded cuffs. It doesn't take much imagination to understand its purpose, and the thought alone makes heat bloom low in my stomach.

The next box reveals a gag, one designed to keep my mouth open while muffling sounds, yet carefully constructed not to hinder his ability to fuck my face as he pleases.

The third contains a candy-cane garter, a playful nod to the replica he's used before.

The final box holds lingerie—dark and striking. A black lace bodysuit trimmed with deep red scalloped lace around the cups and hips, with matching dark red boning along the seams. It's surprisingly bold for something meant for Christmas, but the thought of how it would look paired with my black thigh-high stockings sends a thrill through me.

I can already picture the way his gaze will darken when he sees me in it, the way his control might waver for just a moment. The idea of bringing him to his knees has me more excited than I care to admit.

Whoever he is, he has spent so much time asserting his dominance that I want nothing more than to make him bend to *my* will.

With newfound determination, I carefully tucked the gifts away and headed to my library. If tomorrow would be the night he revealed himself, I needed to be ready. I skimmed the shelves for any Christmas-themed books, hoping for ideas that might drive him as wild as he did me.

***

I must have fallen asleep in my library because that's where I woke up—startled by the distinct sensation of a mouth on my pussy. Groggily, I blink, trying to focus. Looking down, I see him—my masked mystery man—on his knees, his face buried between my thighs, feasting on me.

He's wearing his signature mask, paired with a dark shirt that conceals most of his features, keeping him shrouded in shadow and intrigue. I try to focus, but the way his tongue moves against me makes it impossible to think clearly.

Neither of us speak for a moment. He swirls his tongue over my clit in deliberate, maddening circles before sliding two fingers against my entrance, easing them in slowly. A soft moan escapes my lips as I watch him, my curiosity breaking through the haze of pleasure.

"What's your mask supposed to be, anyway?" I manage, my voice breathy and unsteady.

For a moment, he doesn't reply, keeping his mouth on me as his fingers thrust as deep as possible. Then, as he hooks them just right, pulling a gasp from my throat, he finally speaks.

"It's a Krampus mask," he murmurs, his voice low and rough.

I can only nod, pleasure clouding my thoughts. "Do you know the folklore behind him?" he asks, his fingers now moving with calculated precision. I'm putty in his hands—after being unable to cum last time, I'm right at the edge of my release.

"Yes," I breathe, struggling to form coherent words. "He was Saint Nicholas' counterpart... a half-demon who punished misbehaving children."

He pulls his fingers free but doesn't leave me bereft for long, his touch moving to circle my clit again. This time, there's no teasing; the intensity tells me he isn't planning to leave me unsatisfied.

But then I feel the press of his finger somewhere unexpected—against my backside. I jolt, my body stiffening instinctively.

"What are you doing?" I ask, panic lacing my voice.

He doesn't falter. Instead, his touch against my clit grows more deliberate, drawing my focus back to the pleasure coursing through me. "I need you ready for me tomorrow night, little angel," he murmurs, his tone calm but firm.

His words made my eyes widen. "I've never... done that before," I admit, shaking my head.

He tilts his head slightly, as if my confession caught him off guard. For a moment, he's completely still, then groans deeply, his voice thick with desire. "Fuck. You have no idea what that does to me."

I swallow hard as his finger slides up my slit, teasing me before trailing back down to press against the tight, unfamiliar sensation of my untouched, virgin entrance. My breath hitches in my throat, anticipation and nerves warring within me.

"Just breathe," he whispers, his voice softer now, coaxing me.

I force myself to take a shuddering breath, which turns into a moan when his other hand strikes my pussy with a sharp slap, the sting only enhancing the pleasure as his mouth descends on me once more.

When he sucks my clit into his mouth, his finger presses in deeper, using the distraction to ease past the initial resistance. The slow, deliberate thrusts of his finger are surprisingly gentle, coaxing my body to relax around him.

The combination of his tongue and his touch send me spiraling into a haze of sensation, my muscles beginning to unclench as I surrender to him.

As soon as he feels my body relax around his finger, he presses in a second. This time, he reaches to the side and produces a small bottle. The cold sensation of liquid on his fingers, still seated deep inside me, makes me jolt, and I realize it's lube.

I glare at him, exhaling sharply. "Where was that before you started?"

He chuckles, low and smooth, his tone effortlessly infuriating. "I needed to know you were willing first."

The next thrust feels different—deeper, slicker. The slight edge of pain begins to fade, replaced by an unusual fullness. It isn't exactly pleasure, but something altogether new.

He doesn't give me time to dwell on it. His fingers thrust deeper, curling slightly, as his mouth finds my clit again. The dual sensations make my body hum, every nerve firing under his command. Slowly, the strange fullness morphs into small pulses of pleasure radiating outward. My moans grow louder, unbidden, and my hips start to move with his rhythm.

And then, just as quickly as it began, he pulls his fingers free, leaving me empty.

A soft whimper escapes me before I can stop it. He hears, of course, and his silent laughter vibrates through the space. "Don't worry, my greedy little angel," he murmurs. "I have something else for you."

From beside him, he lifts something small and black, holding it between his fingers. It's the smallest anal plug from the set he gifted me earlier. My thighs clench instinctively as I remember the entire collection of varying sizes.

He tilts the plug, already glistening with lube, and presses it against me. This time, he doesn't use his mouth to distract me; instead, he works my clit with his thumb, his gaze locked on the plug as he slowly commands my body to accept it.

"That's it," he murmurs when it finally slides into place. "Take it."

The stretch is subtle, but it's enough to make me shiver. He leans back to watch, sitting on his heels, his dark eyes drinking in the sight of me writhing beneath him. "Look at you," he growls, his voice thick with satisfaction.

When his thrusts grow harder, his thumb pressing and rubbing in time with his movements, my body responds instinctively, arching into him. Two of his fingers slide into my drenched pussy, curling perfectly, while his free hand toys with the plug.

I groan loudly as he pulls it free, the sensation startling but strangely electrifying. The moan that escapes me is almost guttural as I feel the next plug press against me—bigger, fuller.

The stretch is more intense, but my body begins to yield, warming to the sensation. "Fuck," I gasp, my voice ragged. "Please don't leave me like you did last night."

The low, sinful chuckle that follows makes me blush. "I won't," he promises, his voice a deep whisper that settles over me like a vow.

Relief floods me, though I barely have time to process it. His fingers work my clit faster, the new plug pushing me to the edge of overstimulation. I almost hate how well he knows my body, how easily he manipulates me with pleasure and pain.

"Do not cum until I tell you to," he commands, his voice sharp and certain.

My brows knit together as I fight the building climax. "Why should I wait?" I ask breathlessly.

He doesn't answer immediately, instead pulling the plug free. The emptiness is fleeting; within seconds, the largest plug presses against me. His voice is a dark promise when he finally speaks. "Because you'll cum harder with the pain mixed with the pleasure."

My body trembles, my resolve fraying. "More," I whisper, not entirely sure what I'm asking for.

His response is immediate. He thrusts the plug deeper and replaces his fingers with the candy-cane replica of his cock. The toy stretches me perfectly, its smooth surface gliding in and out as he fucks me harder. Each thrust sends the plug inside me to a new depth, the sting mingling with the pleasure until I'm gasping for air.

"Don't fight it," he growls, his voice thick with hunger.

I feel so full, yet completely empty. My body craves more, desperate to feel him inside me instead of these toys. As if reading my thoughts, he leans down and whispers against my ear, "I need you ready for what I have planned tomorrow."

With that, he quickens his pace, driving the toy harder as his thumb circles my clit relentlessly. The combination is unbearable, my pleasure climbing higher and higher until I'm teetering on the edge.

"Now," he growls. "Cum for me, little angel."

The demand crashes through me, my body obeying instantly. My orgasm rips through me, my moans uncontrollable as wave after wave of ecstasy slams into me. My oncoming scream is muffled as he shoves his fingers into my mouth—the same fingers he just fucked me with. My eyes roll back at the depravity of his actions, my body sings with pleasure as I am pushed to another crashing wave of ecstasy.

Before I can catch my breath, the toys are pulled from me, leaving me momentarily empty. Then I feel it—his tongue, warm and insistent, against my pussy. The stretch of something larger than any of the plugs follows, pushing into me with steady pressure.

The realization hits me like a shock. He's fucking my ass with something more, stretching me further than I thought possible. His groan fills the room as he watches my body struggle to take him.

"Your pussy came on my cock," he growls. "Now your ass will too. I need it stretched and ready for me tomorrow night."

The weight of his words, paired with the unrelenting sensations, sends me over the edge again. My second orgasm crashes into me, more intense than the first. My body is trembling, spent, but he doesn't stop until I'm crying out, my scream muffled as he pushes his fingers into my mouth.

When I finally come down from the high, my body feels boneless, thoroughly used. He leaves only briefly, returning with a wet washcloth to clean me up. As he tends to me, he kisses the inside of my thigh softly, an almost tender gesture that contrasts with the raw intensity of everything that came before.

And then, as silently as he arrived, he's gone, leaving me alone in my library. Sated. Spent. Completely his.

Him

It takes everything in me to leave her little library. The need to claim her is maddening, clawing at the edges of my sanity. My restraint is hanging by a thread, fraying with each second I spend away from her. Even now, as I force myself to retreat, her scent lingers on my skin, wrapping around me like a tether I can't escape. It's intoxicating—her essence, her presence, seeping into me and taunting me, pulling me back toward her with invisible strings.

The taste of her is still fresh on my lips, a tormenting reminder of what I had just done, and more dangerously, of what I denied myself. I feel feral, a beast caged and pacing inside me, snarling against the thin veneer of control I have left. Every fiber of my being screams to turn around, to take her, to dominate what I already know is mine.

But I can't—not yet.

I close my eyes and inhale deeply, trying to replace her scent with the cold night air, to douse the fire she ignites in me. It's no use. She's everywhere. In my mind, in my blood, in my soul. The phantom sounds of her moans echo in my ears, fanning the flames of my desire, pushing me to an edge I never knew existed.

The thought does little to soothe me. She consumes me, her face, her body, her voice—every moment I've had with her runs on an endless loop in my mind. My control is a fragile thing, barely holding under the weight of my obsession.

By the time I reach home, I'm a wreck, my body taut with unresolved need. I step into the shower, letting the scalding water pour over me, hoping it will burn her out of my system. But even here, she's with me. The memory of her taste, her scent, her cries of pleasure—it all overwhelms me.

I give in. My hand moves of its own accord, seeking release. My head falls back against the tiled wall as I picture her beneath me, writhing, begging, taking everything I give her. The thought of her surrender, of her completely mine, drives me to the brink.

My release comes hard and fast, her name a whispered prayer on my lips. But even that is not enough.

As I step out of the shower, towel slung loosely around my hips, the mantra returns, steady and insistent.

Just one more night.

Tomorrow, she will know. Tomorrow, she will be *mine*.

Her

I spent most of the day anxiously cleaning and organizing, trying to distract myself from the whirlwind of thoughts consuming me. I thought maybe reading would help, but it didn't. No matter what I did, my mind kept circling back to tonight—the night I would finally find out who my masked man was. The anticipation had me on edge, my thoughts running rampant.

Who could it be?

How well do I know him? Do I even know him at all?

Eventually, my curiosity spiraled into a guessing game, my mind sifting through faces, voices, and moments. Deep in thought, I don't hear the footsteps approaching behind me.

Standing on my toes, one hand gripping the counter for balance, I reach for a mug on the shelf above the coffee pot. I stretch as far as I can, the hem of my shirt riding up and exposing the curve of my back.

That's when I feel him.

A hard, warm body pressed against mine from behind, his presence enveloping me completely. I freeze as his hips move against me, the undeniable firmness of his growing arousal pressing into the thin fabric of my shorts. My breath hitches, my body caught between surprise and something much deeper.

One large hand grips my hip with bruising force, holding me firmly in place. The other reaches over me effortlessly, grabbing the mug I was struggling to reach. As he does, his arm brushes against mine, and that's when I see them—the tattoos.

I know those lines, those intricate patterns. I've traced them with my eyes too many times to not recognize them now.

It's—

"Damien," I whisper, his name escaping my lips on a shaky breath that turned into a soft, involuntary moan as he presses harder into me.

With the mug in his hand, he spins me around, his movements fluid and commanding. He places the cup in my hand, though it trembles slightly under his intense gaze.

"Fuck," he growls, his voice low and rough. "Why can't I stay away from you?"

Before I can respond, his strong hands grip the backs of my thighs, lifting me as if I weigh nothing. He sets me on the counter and pulls my legs apart to accommodate the powerful frame of his body. His hands settle on my hips, pulling me into him until I can feel every inch of his rigid cock pressing against the wet heat between my legs, and I struggle to stifle a moan.

My hands, trembling but curious, rest on his broad shoulders before sliding down his tattooed chest, tracing the contours of his muscles and over the hard ridges of his abs. I feel him tense under my touch, his restraint hanging by a thread.

Damien leans in, his lips so close I can feel the warmth of his breath on mine. My heart is pounding wildly, and for a brief moment, I feel myself giving in, wanting to close the distance between us.

But I can't.

Just as his lips brush against the corner of my mouth, I turn my head away, breaking the moment. "I'm sorry," I say softly, my voice barely above a whisper. "I can't."

His jaw clenches, the frustration clear in the tension radiating from him. Reluctantly, he steps back, giving me enough space to slide down off the counter. The second my feet hit the ground, I move past him, my guilt threatening to consume me.

I flee to my room, shutting the door behind me and collapsing onto my bed. The tears come fast, hot and unrelenting, as weeks—months—of pent-up emotions spill out all at once.

The frustration of my masked man's hold over me.

The hurt I've buried from my ex.

And the deep, aching guilt I always feel when I turn Damien away.

I've wanted him for so long, but I can't bear the thought of jeopardizing his friendship with my brother. The fear of ruining everything is keeping me at arm's length, no matter how much it hurts.

I cry until exhaustion pulls me under, my body finally surrendering to the sleep I so desperately need.

***

I'm jolted from sleep by the sound of my phone buzzing. Rubbing my eyes, I realize I've only slept for three hours. It's six o'clock now. Grabbing my phone, I see a text from my mystery man.

> Tonight's the night. I'll see you in a few hours.

I don't reply—it doesn't feel like it warrants one. I don't know exactly when he'll arrive, but I do know I need to eat before doing anything else. Since it's Christmas Eve and I don't want to wait for takeout, I decide to cook.

When I step into the kitchen, I notice the living room is empty—not that it's surprising. Jax had gone to the airport to pick up Mom and Dad and told me he'd be staying there tonight. He promised to come by in the morning with coffee to get me. So, for tonight, I have the house to myself.

Once I've cooked my sausage, peppers, and rice, I settle cross-legged on the couch and put on a Christmas movie. This one is about a reporter pretending to be a tutor who falls for a princess but ends up in love with the prince. It's light and cute—exactly what I need before the darker desires of the night take over.

With dinner and the movie done, I quickly clean the kitchen. It's time to start getting ready.

First, I take a shower. I'm not washing my hair, so I tie it up into a messy bun, strip, and step under the hot water. I hadn't realized how tense I was until I felt the heat melt the stiffness from my body. After standing there for a moment, I get to work: scrubbing my body, applying shaving oil, and carefully shaving. When I'm done, I use my favorite rose-scented body wash.

Satisfied, I step out of the shower and smooth on body oil, ensuring my skin is silky smooth while locking in the musky floral scent I love. Wrapping myself in a light black robe, I'm ready to do my hair.

I decide on loose curls that frame my face and cascade over my shoulders, falling halfway down my back. While curling, I think about my makeup. Should I go for a natural look or something darker and smokier to bring out my eyes? I settle on the latter—the darker look will pair better with the outfit he left for me.

Once my smokey eye is finished, I add the same red lipstick that once made him want to *fuck my face in my sleep.* I know he loved it when I left my mark on him. After a final glance in the mirror, I add a thick layer of mascara, imagining how he'll enjoy seeing it streaked down my cheeks later.

The last step is getting dressed, but before that, I check my phone. There's a message from my mystery man, sent twenty minutes ago:

> It's almost time, little angel. I hope you're ready.

Glancing at the clock, I see it's already quarter past ten. I'm thankful the last few hours have flown by, but now I feel like I need to move faster.

I lay the outfit he left for me on the bed along with the stockings and the new garter. A wave of anxiousness washes over me. I don't know exactly what to expect tonight, but I do know I want everything he's prepared to give.

With careful movements, I untie my robe and let it pool at my feet, reaching for the lace bodysuit first. After slipping into it, I pull on the stockings and secure the garter around my right thigh. Once dressed, I stand in front of the full-length mirror.

The outfit is perfect. It pushes up my breasts, making them look fuller, while the boning in the bodysuit pulls in my waist, emphasizing my hourglass figure. The dark lace contrasts beautifully against my ivory skin. Staring at my reflection, I decide to pull some of my hair back, leaving loose curls to frame my face while keeping most of it flowing down my back.

The final look is sultry, giving off the vibe of a mistress stolen away by Krampus—his to punish and claim. It's exactly what I want.

Satisfied, I pull the robe back on, leaving it loosely tied. Gathering the gifts I've prepared, I take them downstairs and arrange them under the tree. Finally, I position myself beneath the tree, waiting for my mystery man to arrive.

Her

To my utter surprise, I don't have to wait long. Butterflies erupt in my stomach when I hear the front door open. With a clear view of the entryway, I see him the moment he steps inside. His presence sucks all the air from my lungs. After shutting the door, he locks it behind him, then turns his full attention to me. His gaze scorches a deliberate path along my skin. Frozen in place, I sit there, taking him in.

The black button-up shirt clings to his muscular frame, tapering perfectly at his waist and tucked neatly into a pair of fitted black slacks. He's paired the ensemble with black Converse, an unexpected touch that somehow works. The mask he wears makes him even more imposing. Every deliberate, slow step he takes toward me makes it harder to catch my breath.

When he finally stops in front of me, he extends a gloved hand—the one not hidden behind his back. Without a word, he helps me to my feet. Standing so close, he towers over me, his intense gaze never wavering. Slowly, his fingers loosen the tie around my waist before teasing their way up the curve of my body. They trail over my breast, making my nipples harden, then slide over my collarbone before his hand settles firmly around my throat.

His voice, low and commanding, sends a shiver down my spine.

"Are you gifting yourself to me, little angel?" he asks, his tone smooth and deliberate.

All I can manage is a small nod, completely entranced by him. He chuckles softly, a sound that's both teasing and dark.

"In that case, I think I'd like it better without the robe," he murmurs, leaning in. The feathers of his mask tickle my ear as his voice hardens. "Lose the fucking robe."

His tone leaves no room for argument.

He steps back just enough to give me space to comply. My hands move to untie the robe, letting it slip off my shoulders and pool on the floor at my feet. Only then does he release my throat, taking another step back to survey me. His eyes rake over me slowly, and I take the opportunity to do the same. My gaze catches on the growing bulge in his slacks, heat blooming low in my belly.

When I finally tear my eyes away, his amusement is unmistakable.

"Like what you see?" he asks, a slow, smoky laugh rumbling in his chest.

I roll my eyes, earning myself another chuckle. Looking up at him through my lashes, I shrug lightly.

"I haven't really seen enough to know yet," I reply, feigning indifference.

He shakes his head at me, his lips curving into a smirk. Then, finally, he reveals the hand he's kept behind his back.

"I thought you might like one last gift."

In his hand is a collar. A fucking collar.

Before I can fully process the sight of it, he closes the distance between us in two swift strides. His hand shoots out, gripping my throat again with just the right amount of pressure. As he steps into me, I instinctively back away, my spine meeting the wall behind me. His breath is warm against my ear when he whispers, "Why do you think I chose the Krampus mask?"

I shrug slightly, not trusting myself to speak with the way his hand tightens around my neck.

"Your collar suits you," he continues, holding it up for me to see. The black band is adorned with rose gold letters and pink stones, spelling out one word: *Brat*.

It's not a collar I would've chosen for myself, but somehow, it feels perfect.

"Just like this mask suits me," he adds, his voice darkening. "And my need to punish and tame you."

My thighs clench together, heat pooling between them. I need him to do just that.

I stare into the eyes of his mask. This close, I can finally understand why I haven't been able to see his eyes—the material covering them obscures them from view. I can't see him, but he can see me. The tension stretches between us, thick and electric. When his grip on my neck tightens, I finally answer, my voice raspy but deliberate.

"Well, what are you waiting for? It's not going to put itself on, now is it?"

The effect is immediate. He releases my throat, and I take a deep breath, my chest rising and falling rapidly as I watch him. I stay perfectly still while he fastens the collar around my neck. The click of the clasp sends a surge of heat through me, a sense of ownership taking hold.

He steps back slightly, his voice low and full of satisfaction.

"Now, for being such a good fucking slut for me, you deserve a reward."

When his hands move to remove his mask, my breath catches. My entire body freezes, anticipation gripping me in a chokehold. A million thoughts race through my mind as he pushes the mask up, revealing a knowing smirk and a pair of chocolate-brown eyes that leave me speechless.

"Damien?" I breathe, barely audible.

This can't be happening.

The events of the last few weeks flood my mind, crashing over me like a tidal wave. My body remains rooted in place, unable to move or react. He watches me silently, allowing me time to process.

"It was you?" I whisper, disbelief thick in my voice.

He nods, his gaze unwavering. "It's always been me, Anastasia."

He takes a step toward me but halts when I raise my hand, silently asking him to stop. Tears sting my eyes as the weight of realization presses down on me. I've wanted this man for years, but I've always told myself no—for my brother's sake.

"Damien, we can't," I manage to say, looking down to hide the hurt and disappointment on my face.

This time, when he steps closer, I can't bring myself to stop him. My resolve crumbles as I fight to keep my tears at bay.

"Why not, little angel?" he asks, his tone laced with disappointment.

I now understand why he always whispered—it concealed his voice. It's a detail I can't unhear now.

"Give me one good reason," he presses, his frustration clear.

Swallowing hard, I force the words out. "My brother. I can't jeopardize his friendship with you."

His sigh is one of pure relief, confusing me.

Gently, he tilts my chin up, forcing me to meet his gaze. "Is that the only thing stopping you from being mine?" he asks, his voice soft yet commanding.

A small whimper escapes me at the thought of being his. I nod, swallowing past the lump in my throat. "I would never forgive myself," I admit, my voice trembling.

To my surprise, a smile breaks across his face.

"Why are you smiling?" I ask, furrowing my brows.

His smile only widens. "Because, brat, I finally told him how I feel about you. How I've felt all these years. And how I was worried it might ruin our friendship, so I tried to ignore it."

His gaze searches mine, as if looking for confirmation that I feel the same.

"Anyway," he continues, "we talked about it. He told me that if I truly wanted to be with you—and if I thought I could make you happy—he wouldn't stand in the way."

His hand moves to cup my cheek, his touch so gentle it sends a fresh wave of tears to my eyes.

Leaning into his hand, I meet his gaze, searching for any hint of doubt. "You're saying he's okay with this? With us?"

He nods, brushing a stray tear from my cheek. "Yes. If that's what you want."

His words settle over me like a balm, soothing my nerves. It *is* what I want.

"Wait," I say suddenly, narrowing my eyes at him. "When did you talk to him?"

He shakes his head, clearly amused by my skepticism. "About a week after everything happened with my brother."

"Why didn't you tell me?" I demand.

His lips quirk into a smirk. "Because this was more fun. And now, if you're done being a brat, I'm going to kiss you."

His hand moves from my cheek to the back of my neck, pulling me closer until our lips brush. It's a whisper of a kiss, soft and teasing, before his grip on my hip tightens. My answering moan is all the invitation he needs.

His tongue slides against mine, the kiss deepening into a battle of dominance I know I'm destined to lose. Still, I fight for it, even as his control over me becomes inevitable.

Him

She tastes so fucking sweet, and I know I'll never get enough of her. The way her lips mold to mine is intoxicating. I pull back slightly, smiling. She narrows her eyes at me.

"Something funny?" she snaps, all attitude—the way I like her.

My smile widens. "A couple of things, actually." I lean in to kiss her nose, enjoying the way her cheeks flush in response.

"Care to enlighten me?" she asks, dodging my next attempt to kiss her.

My patience thins; I've waited far too long to claim her as mine. "First, you pretty much admitted you love me."

Her blush deepens, spreading like wildfire. Before she can say anything, I reach out, my hand wrapping around her delicate neck.

"Second," I continued, tightening my grip slightly, "it's cute that you think you have any control here."

I pull her closer, my tongue running along the seam of her lips. When she parts them, granting me entry, I take what's mine before pushing her backward. She stumbles into the wooden chair near the tree, and with a firm hand on her shoulder, I press her down into it. The power shift is palpable. I kneel before her, and from the way she bites her lip, I can tell she loves seeing me on my knees for her.

But not yet.

Tearing my gaze away, I search for what I saw earlier among the scattered items. My hand closes around it—a length of bondage tape lying between the remote toy and the gag.

With it in hand, I stand, circling her like a predator stalking its prey.

"Hands behind you, little angel," I order, my tone firm.

She doesn't move, defiance gleaming in her eyes. Testing me.

I grab a fistful of her hair, forcing her head back so she has no choice but to look up at me. "Now is not the time to be a brat," I warn, tightening my grip slightly.

She winces, a mischievous smile curving her lips. She's pushing me, and she knows exactly what she's doing. Running my free hand down her cheek, I hear her soft whimper—a sound that tells me everything I need to know. She craves this, the loss of control, the surrender. And I'm going to give it to her.

"I came here to make your dark desires come true," I murmur, my lips brushing her ear. "The ones you read about in those books of yours. I've seen you get yourself off to them, remember? I even gave you the shirt I came all over, so you'd think of me while you did it."

Her breath hitches, and she nods slightly, her blush returning.

Wrapping my hand tighter around her throat, I continue. "And I'll let you in on a little secret. I've been keeping track of the books you read here—then reading them myself."

Her eyes widen, surprise flickering across her face.

"That's right. I know every depraved thing you want done to you. And trust me, I'm going to do them." My voice lowers. "But first, you're going to put your hands behind your fucking back."

She glares at me, stubborn as always, but slowly moves her arms behind her.

"Good fucking girl," I praise, loosening my grip and pressing a kiss to her hair. She squirms in the chair at the sound of my approval, and I smirk, knowing exactly how to get under her skin.

Making quick work of binding her wrists with the bondage tape, I test it to make sure she won't be able to escape. Once satisfied, I head back to the tree, grabbing the leg spreader I spotted earlier.

"Just one more thing," I tell her as I kneel to secure her ankles.

Her glare returns, but her silence speaks louder—she wants this. She always has.

With her legs spread open before me, I can't help myself. My hand moves to her clit, rubbing it through the thin fabric of her outfit. Her soft moans fuel my need, and I press harder, drawing deeper sounds from her.

"I'm not stopping this time," I tell her, my voice a low growl. I rise to meet her gaze, hooking a finger under the collar around her neck and pulling her toward me.

Her eyes are wide, pupils dilated. She's completely at my mercy.

"But before we go any further," I say, toying with the letters on her collar, "you need to trust me."

I pause, watching her carefully.

"The other night—when you stopped me—I was going to make you cum harder than you ever have. Your safe word is 'mistletoe.' From now on, if anything ever becomes too much, say it, and I'll stop immediately. But that's the only way I'm stopping. Got it?"

She nods, but it's not enough. My hand finds her throat again, tilting her head back so she has no choice but to meet my eyes.

"Words, little angel. I need your words. Do you understand?"

"Yes," she says quickly, her voice trembling but sure. "Yes, I understand."

I release her throat, nodding in satisfaction. "Good girl."

Now that we're on the same page, I undo the snaps between her thighs. The moment I see her glistening pussy—bound, aching and ripe for the picking as she is—I lose all control.

I'm on her in an instant, my mouth devouring her, my fingers plunging inside her. Her moans fill the air, each one fueling my hunger.

They're for me. Not for some anonymous, masked man. *Me.*

The man who has craved her for five long years.

Looking up at her, our eyes lock, and I hook my fingers inside her, finding that spot that makes her unravel. Her head falls back, a guttural moan tearing from her throat.

"Fuck, Damien. Don't stop. Please."

Hearing my name spill from her lips like that, drenched in pleasure, ignites something feral inside me. I need to hear it again. There's no chance I'm stopping tonight.

I lift my mouth from her for only a moment to murmur, "I don't plan on it," before latching back onto her clit, sucking hard.

Her scream of pleasure is music to my ears, and when I feel her walls begin to clench around my fingers, I quicken my movements, pushing her closer to the edge. My free hand reaches down, searching for the smallest plug I'd prepared earlier. Feeling how slick she's made my chin and fingers, I know she's more than ready for it.

Pressing the toy against her tight entrance, I hear her moan—a new, raw sound I wasn't expecting, one that makes my cock ache. As it begins to slide in, her body tenses for only a moment before she starts rocking into my touch, panting as it slips into place.

"Fuck, your tight little ass took that so nicely," I praise, the words pulling an answering moan from her.

"Yes," she pants, her voice growing desperate. "Fuck. I'm going to cum."

She looks down at me, wild and undone. "Don't you dare fucking stop."

I don't. How could I?

"Cum for me, little angel," I demand, my voice low and rough, as I release the plug and focus entirely on her clit. My tongue and fingers drive her higher until her body finally gives in, shattering beneath my touch.

"Fuck, Damien, it's happening again," she gasps, her hips grinding against my hand.

Her climax crashes over her, a sheen of sweat glistening on her flushed skin. Her cries echo around us, and I hum in approval, slowing my movements to guide her down gently.

"You cum so beautifully for me," I murmur, leaning forward to press a kiss against her trembling thigh.

She's still catching her breath when I carefully swap the plug for the next size, watching her body adjust, her lips parted in a soft gasp. Standing with a need to feel her, I untie her hands and pull her to her feet, her legs still bound. Her body melts into mine as I kiss her, hard and demanding, forcing her to taste herself on my tongue. Her answering moans tell me everything I need to know.

But it's not enough.

When she goes to deepen the kiss, I pull back, smirking at her protest, and shove my damp fingers into her mouth. She gags slightly, the sound shooting straight to my cock.

"Not so defiant now, are you?" I taunt, using the leverage to press her down to her knees.

"You know," I begin, my voice a low growl, "last night, I almost gave in. On the way home, I could still taste you on my lips. It drove me insane."

Her tongue glides across my fingers, her eyes never leaving mine.

"I had to shower, worried your scent would pull me back to you. I couldn't stop thinking about you."

I pull my fingers from her mouth, and she immediately moves to unbutton my pants, quick and eager. While she works, I shrug off my shirt, letting it fall to the ground. She pushes my pants down, freeing my aching cock, and her eyes widen slightly in surprise.

"You pierced your dick?" she asks, amusement flickering through her lust-filled gaze.

I grip myself, stroking slowly. "I did. It's called the magic cross."

Before I can say more, her tongue darts out, swiping the bead of pre-cum from the tip. Her mouth teases the four beads of the piercing, her lips curling into a wicked smile as she takes me in inch by inch, testing the metal.

She moves slowly at first, her lips soft and wet, but the moment she wraps her hand around the base, cupping my balls, I feel her relax, taking me deeper. My hand slides into her hair, gathering it in a fist, tipping her head back just enough to meet my gaze.

"If it gets too much, tap my thigh twice," I tell her firmly.

She nods, her eyes flashing with that familiar defiance.

I start slow, thrusting deep and steady, holding her in place before pulling back to let her catch her breath. But it doesn't take long before I'm fucking her face, my pace quickening as her mascara smudges and tears cling to her lashes.

"Fuck, Anastasia," I groan, her name spilling from my lips as her throat tightens around me.

Her eyes meet mine, wet and fiery, refusing to yield. I slow, teasing her, letting the tension coil tighter and tighter. Sliding my cock deep into her throat, I hold it there, watching her struggle to take me. She gags, her throat convulsing around me, and I pull back long enough for her to gasp for air.

"That's it, little angel," I growl, thrusting back into her heat. "Swallow that fucking cock."

She takes me again, her hands gripping my thighs as her throat works around me. Each bob of her head, each flick of her tongue, drives me closer to the edge, but I hold back. Not yet.

When I finally pull away, her lips are swollen, her cheeks flushed, and she looks up at me with unrestrained hunger.

"I need to be inside you now," I tell her, my voice rough with need.

Him

I yank her off my glistening cock, her saliva trailing in strings from her lips to me. She gasps as I pull her up, her legs wobbling slightly before she finds her footing. Taking a seat on the couch, I lean forward, unclasping one of the cuffs from the spreader bar. Sitting back, I give her a steady look.

"For taking my cock so well into your mouth," I say, my voice low, "I want you to sit on it."

Her eyes light up with eagerness as she positions herself over me, her hands on my shoulders for balance. I rest my head back against the couch, taking her in. "Now's your chance to use me for your pleasure," I tell her, deliberately not moving to line myself up.

She hesitates briefly before grasping my shaft, guiding me to her entrance. Slowly, she sinks down, inch by inch, her breath hitching as I stretch her.

"Oh, fuck, you're so big," she breathes, her voice quivering.

Her pace is slow as her body adjusts, but when she finally takes me to the hilt, I curse under my breath. "Fuck, angel. Keep that up, and I won't last. You're so fucking tight."

She leans forward, her forehead resting against mine, both of us breathing heavily. I let her take the lead, my hands simply resting on her thighs, occasionally gripping them when the pleasure surges. I savor the sight of her, the way her face contorts with need and frustration as she struggles to take enough of me to satisfy herself.

"Are you just going to sit there?" she snaps, her bratty tone cutting through the haze of desire.

I shrug, smirking at her. "I've waited years for this, angel. If I were in control the way I want to be right now, my piercings would hurt you. As much as I enjoy mixing pain with your pleasure, I won't do it like this."

Her defiance flares, and she reaches between us, her fingers sliding toward her clit. Instinct takes over. My hand shoots out, capturing both of hers in one grip while the other smacks her breast, hard enough to make her gasp.

"Is this what you wanted?" I growl, my control starting to slip as her pussy clenches around me.

"Yes," she moans, arching into the sting of my hand as it strikes her other breast. "This is what I want."

Her hips move faster now, chasing the pleasure, and I reach up, wrapping my hand around her throat. I squeeze just enough to remind her who's in charge, then start pounding into her mercilessly. The way she tightens around me, her cries growing louder with every thrust, snaps the last thread of my restraint.

"Fuck, you know how to get under my skin," I groan.

In one swift motion, I lift her off my lap and flip her onto her back, pressing her into the couch. She's breathless and flushed, her eyes blazing with need as I reattach her ankle to the spreader bar.

"You might get under my skin," I say, stepping back to take her in, "but I'm still the one in control here."

She looks wrecked—her legs forced open, the bodysuit bunched around her waist, red marks blooming on her breasts, makeup smeared, and her collar glinting in the dim light. She's mine, completely undone beneath me.

Stroking my cock, I relish the way her juices make my hand slick. "Look at you," I murmur. "So used already. So needy for me. And we've only just started."

Grabbing the largest plug—a replica of my cock—and a bottle of lube, I move back to the couch. Lifting the bar with one hand, I slide her to the edge, her body trembling with anticipation. I toy with the smaller plug already inside her, pushing and pulling until it glides easily. Her moans start low and desperate, growing louder as her body relaxes.

When I press the larger one to her entrance, she tenses, her eyes wide with a mix of trepidation and desire.

Knowing she needs more, I lift the bar over my shoulders, spreading her legs even further as I lower my mouth to her soaked pussy. My tongue flicks her clit, teasing and tasting her, drawing out a symphony of moans. Her body begins to writhe, her hips bucking toward me as the tension coils tighter and tighter inside her.

Just as she's on the edge, I pause, reaching for the glistening silicone toy. But her voice cuts through my focus.

"No," she pleads, her voice hoarse with need. "I want you."

Her desperation makes my cock twitch, but I offer her a warning. "It may hurt," I say, watching her closely.

She furrows her brow, confused, and I sigh, leaning closer. "I've wanted this for too long to be gentle, angel. Once I'm inside you like this, I won't stop. I'll fuck you."

A shudder runs through her at my words, the plug sliding deeper inside as her body clenches.

"I don't care," she whispers, her voice trembling. "I need you."

Her raw honesty breaks the last barrier between us, but I need her to understand. "I will fuck you hard," I say, my voice dark with promise, "hard enough to leave my mark inside you."

She nods, her hands sliding up her body to play with her nipples through the lace covering them.

"Now, Damien," she demands, her voice fierce and needy.

I position myself at her entrance, teasing her clit with the barbells of my piercing, savoring the way she trembles. "Hard enough that you'll feel me long after I'm gone," I growl.

"Do it," she breathes. "Now."

And I give her exactly what she asked for.

With a sharp movement forward, she gasps, the sound caught somewhere between pleasure and pain—either way, I'm not stopping. Her legs still rest on my shoulders as I grip the thin of her waist, holding her steady against me. The way her body moves in rhythm with mine is intoxicating, and I lose myself in the moment.

"No man will ever fill you the way I do," I honest-to-God moan. "The mark of my piercing will be so deep in your pussy, no man or toy will measure up."

She tightens around me, fueled by my words, but her voice cuts through the haze. "Damien, it hurts," she says, her tone soft yet raw.

I pause, looking into her eyes, unsure whether to continue. She interrupts my hesitation. "No! Don't stop! I like it."

A slow smirk spreads across my face as I lean in closer, my voice low. "You were fucking made for this. For *me*." I adjust my pace to make it almost punishing, attentive to every response her body gives, determined to make the pain as good as she needs, to deliver the pleasure she craves.

Her breathing quickens, her body tensing as she nears her peak. Her cunt grips me tightly, milking my cock with an almost overwhelming intensity. Her voice drops to a whisper, filled with a need she can't seem to contain. "More. I need more."

I nod, cupping her face gently. "I've got you, baby girl. Just trust me, okay?" She nods, her trust absolute, and it fuels my resolve to guide her where she wants to go.

I remove the toy, before spreading some lube on my throbbing cock. I take my time, ensuring her comfort, rubbing her clit with my thumb and whispering encouragement as she adjusts to every shift and sensation. "Good girl," I murmur, kissing her softly, anchoring her with my presence. "Your ass is taking my cock so well. Just keep breathing, little angel, the piercings will be the worst part." True to my words, as soon as the piercings touch her walls, she winces.

I turn my head, kissing her calf softly as she relaxes for me. "You are doing so good," I murmur the praise she deserves, grabbing the replicated toy and pressing the head into her dripping pussy, testing, as I slowly work my dick inside her.

"Fuck, seeing you this stretched for me is almost too much," I groan, my control slipping from me at the beautiful view.

I keep pushing the toy in, inch by torturous inch, until it's fully seated inside her and she's begging for me.

"Please, Damien," she whines, and my name on her lips sounds fucking divine. "I need more. I'm so close."

My needy little angel moves her legs, causing the toy and my dick to stretch her further, and I can't hold back any longer. I move.

As the tension builds between us, her body responds instinctively, moving in time with mine. Her whispered pleas and the heat of her gaze drive me closer to the edge, but I stay focused on her, my thumb now on her clit to bring her closer to the edge.

"More," she cries out desperately. "Oh shit, Damien. Harder," she demands, and I don't hesitate to give her exactly what she wants.

My hips snap forward, sinking all the way into her tight, squeezing hole and I groan.

"Fuck, angel, your ass is choking my cock so fucking hard."

She starts to tremble, her eyes fluttering shut as her body moves involuntarily. "Fuck, I'm coming," she screams and a shiver runs through her, and she grips both the toy and me tightly.

Fucking beautiful.

I stay focused, determined to chase my own release as her movements grow more intense. Her eyes roll back slightly, her mouth opening in a silent cry of release.

I have a feeling I know what's coming. I quickly remove the toy and replace it with my own dick, increasing the intensity—fucking her harder, rubbing her clit in tighter circles. She presses her hands against my abdomen, a weak attempt to steady herself. I adjust, pulling out until only the head is inside her pussy, and her body responds with a sharp jolt, her release turning into an explosion as she squirts all over me, making a mess of both of us.

Leaning in, I claim her lips with a kiss so deep it leaves us both breathless. When I pull back, I murmur, "That's it. Let go. Soak my fucking cock with your juices." Her chest rises and falls as she catches her breath, her hands trembling slightly.

I hook my finger into her collar and pull her gently toward me. "You look beautiful when you're coming for me," I say softly, brushing my tongue along her lips until she parts them for me. The kiss that follows is slow and consuming, leaving us both dizzy.

When we break apart, I take control, guiding her into the position I want her in. "You had your fun," I whisper, "now it's my turn."

My hand brushes against the last item I grabbed earlier, the gag. A deep need to assert my control burns within me. The collar marks her as mine, her virgin ass may be mine as well, but I feel like I need more—a tangible symbol of her surrender.

Once she's on her knees, I instruct, "Hands on the back of the couch." She moves slower this time but complies without hesitation. Securing the gag quickly, I press a kiss to her shoulder, lining up my dick to her entrance and whisper, "Good girl."

Her movements are instinctive now, her body responding to every cue I give. I pull her head roughly to the side by her hair, leaning close to whisper, "You are mine to use."

Time slows as I snap my hips forward and she nods. My mind sharpens on every detail—her trembling breaths, the way she moves to meet me, the soft sounds of surrender she makes. My release is close, I can feel it, so I slow down to prolong the moment a little while longer.

She pushes her hips back into me, silently pleading for more, and I wrap my arms around her. One hand tweaks her nipple, as the other heads south, and she groans when I make contact with her overused clit.

"You've given me so much tonight," I murmur, my voice low. "But I need just a little more. Come for me one more time." I watch as she takes in my words, her body relaxing in response, trusting me completely as a broken moan leaves her throat.

Her hands falter, and I reach out to steady her. Removing the gag carefully, I let my hand linger on her cheek. "Next time," I say with a faint smirk, "it'll stay on longer." For now, though, I need to hear her voice.

"Say my name," I urge, my tone commanding as I toy with her swollen clit once more. My thrusts turn into a punishment, the pace brutal and I wrap my fingers around her neck.

Her lips part, her breath catching as I squeeze, and she moans, "Use me."

My resolve crumbles.

The release I was holding back is taking over me now, my rhythm lost, my movements jerky. "Fuck. I'm cumming," I roar, the feeling so intense I get lightheaded as I fill her to the brim.

Feeling my hot cum inside her pussy has my little angel clenching around me again.

"Shit, I can feel you twitching, filling me up."

Her words paint images in my mind, ones of her pregnant with my child, her belly swollen. Mine completely.

As the moment reaches its peak, I lean close again, my mouth against the shell of her ear. "You're mine, brat. And I *will* make you mine in every sense of the word," I whisper, my words carrying a promise I plan on fulfilling.

Her

Last night was amazing. My body aches in all the best ways. He used me—fucked every hole—exactly how I'd always craved. And he didn't just take; he made me feel cherished, every step of the way. No judgment, no hesitation, just him giving me everything I'd ever wanted. I loved every second of it.

Peeling my eyes open, I realize I'm back in my bed, under the covers—and alone. My heart races as I sit up, scanning the room for any sign of Damien. Panic starts to bubble up until I spot his clothes and mask sitting on the vanity across the room. Relief washes over me, and I smile to myself at the sight of his things, already referring to him in my mind as my man.

I grab my robe and head off to find him.

I don't have to look far. He's in the kitchen, forever shirtless, standing over the waffle maker. Without even turning around, he says, "Take a picture—it'll last longer." His voice is laced with amusement, and I can practically hear the smirk on his lips.

I roll my eyes, biting back a smile. "Whatever," I say, heading for the coffee pot, determined to ignore the huge elephant in the room: I just slept with my brother's best friend. And I have no idea what that means now.

Before I can grab a mug, Damien slides one into my hand, already filled with fresh, steaming coffee. "I was about to bring you breakfast," he says, nodding toward the tray piled high with food on the counter.

"Oh... thanks," I manage, caught off guard by the gesture.

But before I can retreat back into my head, Damien crowds my space. He plucks the mug from my hand, setting it behind him. His eyes are locked on mine. "What's going on in that head of yours?" he asks, his voice soft but firm.

"Nothing," I lie, shaking my head.

"Bullshit, Ana," he presses, stepping closer, his hands planting on the counter on either side of me. "I know you better than that. What. Is. It? Don't make me ask again." His tone leaves no room for evasion.

I drop my gaze, but he doesn't let me hide. His fingers tilt my chin up, forcing me to meet his eyes. "Fine," I sigh, straightening my spine. "After last night... where does that leave us?"

He searches my face, his lips tugging into a small, knowing smile.

"Glad to see you find this so amusing," I mutter, shoving lightly at his chest, needing some space.

But Damien doesn't budge. Instead, he grabs me, lifting me onto the counter so we're at eye level. "Listen to me, Brat," he says, stepping between my legs, his voice suddenly serious. "I told you last night—I plan to make you mine. In every sense of the word."

His words make my heart race. Before I can respond, he pulls me into a slow, deliberate kiss. His hands grip my hips, hard enough to bruise, as we lose ourselves in the moment. When he starts to pull away, I tug him back, wrapping my arms around his neck.

Damien deepens the kiss, his hand tangling in my hair, pulling just enough to tear our lips apart. But he doesn't stop there—his mouth moves to my neck, kissing, licking, biting a trail that has me moaning his name.

"Damien..." I whisper as he drags me to the edge of the counter, his hard length pressing against me through his sweatpants.

But then he stops, resting his forehead against mine. His hands catch my wandering fingers before they can slip into the waistband of his pants.

"As much as I want to lay you out on this counter and make you scream my name, we can't," he murmurs. "Jaxson's on his way over, and while he might be okay with us, I doubt he'd appreciate seeing the things I'd do to you right now."

A wave of disappointment crashes over me, and he notices, his lips curving into a mischievous smile.

"Later," he promises, stealing one last kiss. What starts as a peck quickly turns heated when I pull him closer, but we're interrupted by the sound of the front door opening.

Jaxson's voice cuts through the tension. "As happy as I am for you two, I don't care who you are—I don't need to see my baby sister playing tongue twister with anyone." He gags for dramatic effect before adding, "Mom and Dad want us home in a few hours, Ana. You'd better get ready."

Damien steps back, helping me down from the counter as Jaxson disappears down the hall.

When I move to head upstairs, Damien stops me with a pointed look at the food. "Eat first."

The tone in his voice leaves no room for argument, and my stomach betrays me with a loud growl. Sheepishly, I sit down, letting him serve me. Only when he's satisfied that I've eaten enough does he let me go.

"I'll clean up here and join you in a few minutes," he says.

I rush upstairs, brushing my teeth and starting the shower. Just as I step under the water, Damien walks into the bathroom, unapologetically naked, his eyes raking over me with unfiltered desire.

He steps into the shower, crowding me instantly. Turning me to face the cool glass, he presses his front against my back. My breath catches as I see our reflection, his hard cock nestled between my thighs.

"You'd look sexy as fuck with these pierced," he murmurs, his hand grazing my nipples before trailing lower. His other arm wraps around my neck, holding me in place as he grips his cock at the base, running it through my wet pussy to gather the moisture pooling there. He slides inside me, painfully slow. I wince at the ache—still sore from last night.

"Fuck, Ana," he groans in my ear. "You take me so well. Even after everything, you're still so eager for me to fill your pussy again."

His filthy words ignite something in me, and I push back against him, but my control is short-lived.

"It's cute you think this happens on your terms," he growls, his grip tightening on my hips as he takes over. "You're mine—remember that. Mine to fucking use."

His pace grows brutal, each thrust pushing me closer to the edge, and I watch it all happen through the glass. When I finally shatter, my moans muffled against his arm, he slows, his voice rough in my ear.

"Where do you want it?" he asks, his release not far behind mine.

"Inside," I whisper, still lost in the throes of pleasure. "I need to feel you cum inside me again."

He groans, driving into me one last time as he spills inside me.

After a moment, he leans in close. "Are you on the pill?"

I nod weakly, still feeling his cock twitching inside me.

"Not anymore, you're not," he says, pulling back just enough to look me in the eye. "I told you—I want all of you. That includes putting my baby in you."

His words leave me breathless, caught off guard from the novel concept of pregnancy, but I don't hesitate. I nod.

"If that's what you want," he whispers, searching for confirmation in my gaze.

I don't even need to think twice. He'd never say such a thing lightly. "It is."

His lips curve into a satisfied smile as he kisses my nose. "Good. Now, we'd better get ready. Don't want to keep your parents waiting."

I watch him step out of the shower, handing me a towel. Looking at my reflection in the mirror, the marks he's left on my body tell me everything I need to know: he's mine, and I'm his.

Him

After our conversation in the shower, my little angel seems happier than ever. I'm still shocked she agreed to stop her birth control. That was a big step, but it feels like everything else will be easier now. Like I told Jaxson, I've been in love with her for a while. She's admitted it twice already—now it's my turn.

She was surprised when she found out I'd be joining them for Christmas dinner. It's not just about our new relationship but also because of what I did to my brother not that long ago. I'm not exactly eager to sit at that table, but Jaxson was quick to invite me, knowing I had plans to tell his sister how I feel about her. Though, to be honest, I haven't really told her yet. That's happening tonight.

On the way there, she turns in her seat, her expression serious. "Damien, I don't want them to know about us yet. They just got back to the country, and I don't want to deal with a barrage of uncomfortable questions. Can we keep it to ourselves, just for today?" She pouts, knowing full well I don't like the idea.

"Just for dinner," she adds, her voice softer. "Then I'm yours to do whatever you want with when we get home."

I stay silent as we pull into the driveway, her words still hanging in the air. Once we park, I unbuckle my seatbelt and lean over the center console. Wrapping my fingers around her delicate neck, I squeeze gently, pulling her attention fully to me. Leaning closer, I let my tongue glide over the shell of her ear before I whisper, "You've got five hours, little angel. Five hours before I take you home and remind you exactly who you belong to."

She squirms in her seat, a quiet moan escaping her lips.

"Yes, please," she breathes.

I release her neck, grabbing her phone. Setting a timer for five hours, I switch it to vibrate and place it back in her hand.

"Five hours," I repeat firmly before stepping out of the car. Walking around to her side, I open the door for her, ready to face whatever this night brings.

***

Dinner was uneventful, just like any other holiday gathering at her family's house—except for the gifts. The timer went off, and my little angel blushed, discreetly silencing it before turning back to Amara, who had only been there for less than forty-five minutes. No doubt, Amara was telling her everything she had observed so far. From the way Amara kept glancing at me, I could tell she wasn't sure how to feel, which confirmed my suspicion: Ana hadn't told her about the last twelve days.

I gave her a few more moments, knowing she wouldn't leave if she thought Amara was upset with her. When I caught her eye, she understood her time was up. She hugged Amara, then the rest of her family, offering a polite excuse for why we needed to leave. As she finished her goodbyes, I retrieved her jacket, and soon, we were out the door.

She moves to open the car door, but I grab her wrist, spinning her around and pressing her back against it. Before I can say anything, she pulls me to her, her free hand clutching my shirt as she rises onto her toes to kiss me. It's messy, urgent, and filled with the need we share for each other. Before I can deepen the kiss, she pulls away slightly, her breath warm against my lips.

"Take me home," she whispered, her voice trembling. "I'm ready to be yours in every way."

Her words sent a jolt through me. I left one last lingering kiss on her lips before stepping back to open the door for her.

Once we're in the car and buckled, I drive toward her house. She seems lost in thought, her gaze distant as she stares out the window. I reach over, taking her hand in mine. "Everything okay with you and Amara?" I ask softly.

With a heavy sigh, she rests her head against the seat. "I think so. She's upset I didn't tell her everything, but she knows how I feel about you. I think she understands."

I squeeze her hand gently. "She just needs a little time. You two will be fine."

She turns to me, her eyes meeting mine. "I know. I just hate it when she's upset with me."

I hum in understanding, letting her process her emotions. "And thank you," she adds after a moment, her voice quieter. "For giving me the time to make sure we were okay. I don't think I could've enjoyed tonight if I thought she was still mad at me."

I smirk, pulling her hand to my lips and kissing it softly. "I know," I say, my tone teasing. "That's why I gave you the extra time."

The rest of the drive is quiet, a comfortable silence between us. I want her to have the space she needs to clear her thoughts, so when we get back to her house, she won't be distracted.

Fifteen minutes later, we pulled up to her place. She blinks, seeming to snap out of her daze as she realizes we've arrived. Before she can open the door, I'm there, offering her my hand. She steps out, her smile soft but full of emotion, and it makes my heart race.

"What are you waiting for?" she teases when I hesitate, her tone light but inviting.

"Nothing," I reply, my voice dropping as I let my gaze roam over her. "Just thinking about how beautiful you'll look wearing my marks."

Her small gasp is all the confirmation I needed.

Inside, I lock the door, my movements deliberate as I turn to face her. "Now," I murmur, closing the distance between us, "let's take a look at my canvas."

She backs away slowly, retreating until her hips bump into the kitchen island. I cross the distance in three long strides, pressing her back against the countertop. Leaning down, I run my tongue along the length of her neck, savoring the way she shivers beneath me.

"I think I'll fuck you right here. Do you know how many mornings I wanted to bend you over this counter?" I whisper into her ear.

She shakes her head, her breath hitching.

Gripping her waist, I spin her around, pressing her upper body down onto the cool surface. My hips follow, pinning her in place as I grind my throbbing cock against her backside, coaxing a moan from her lips.

"Just like this," I growl. "I wanted to push your shorts to the side and take you from behind."

Her breath hitches as I smack her ass, gripping it firmly before pulling her back against me. "Would you have liked that?"

"Yes," she moans, pressing into me, her body pliant beneath my hands.

I grab a fistful of her hair, pulling her upright so her back is flush against my chest. She turns her head, capturing my lips in a kiss that's all teeth and tongue, desperate and consuming. When I bite her bottom lip, she moans, her surrender fueling my need.

I don't have the patience I had last night. I need her now.

My hands work quickly, pulling her sweater dress up her body. Our kiss breaks only long enough for her to tug it over her head before our lips fuse again, hungry and desperate. Her hands move with practiced ease, unbuttoning my shirt as I reach around to unclasp her bra. When her fingers reach for my zipper, I halt her, leaning down to grab her thighs and lift her onto the counter.

Sliding my hands up her bare front, I break the kiss, my lips trailing down her neck, across her collarbone, and over the soft swell of her breasts. When I reach one nipple, I scrape it lightly with my teeth, earning me a sharp gasp. My other hand finds her other breast, teasing and tweaking her hardening nipple as I bite down gently.

Her head falls back, cries of pleasure filling the kitchen. The need to claim her consumes me. I take the side of her breast into my mouth, sucking hard, leaving my mark before moving to the other side and doing the same. Pride fills me at the marks left on her beautiful skin.

"Oh, fuck," she breathes, her voice trembling. She knows exactly what I was doing.

The need to taste her overtakes me. I grasp her throat gently, pushing her back onto the counter. My lips trail lower, leaving small marks down her stomach. When I reach the waistband of her leggings, I peel them off, revealing bare skin. No panties.

"Fuck me," I groan, the sight of her making my cock ache with need.

She props herself up on her elbows, a sly smirk on her lips. "That's the idea," she taunts, her voice daring me to take what I want.

I step between her legs, lifting one and pressing kisses along her calf, then her thigh. When I reach the sensitive skin near her pussy, I leave a larger, darker mark before moving to the other leg, repeating the process. This time, when I reach her slick heat, I flatten my tongue against her entrance, dragging it up to her clit. I suck it into my mouth, flicking it with my tongue, savoring the way her body writhes beneath me.

"Fuck, yes, Damien!" she moans, my name falling from her lips like a prayer.

Hearing her scream for me unravels the last shred of control I had, my desire turning into a tornado. I free my cock in an instant, the need to claim her overwhelming.

I tear my mouth from her dripping cunt, standing to line myself up with her entrance. My voice is rough, low, as I warn, "I won't go slow for you."

She nods. Her understanding is all the permission I need. My hips snap forward, burying myself inside her in one smooth motion. Her scream of pleasure echoes around us, spurring me on.

"I've waited for this for so long," I groan, gripping her hips as I thrust into her.

Her hands reach for me, desperate to touch any part of me she can. I catch one of her wrists, pulling her up to capture her lips in a fierce kiss. My other hand fishes something out of my pocket, the weight of it grounding me in the moment.

She flattens her palms against my chest, her nails digging into my skin as her voice breaks with a whimper. "I'm close," she breathes.

My pace doesn't falter, her walls fluttering around me. I release her wrist, taking her chin between my fingers and forcing her to meet my gaze. "There's no escaping me," I growl. "You were always the end game for me."

My hand slides to her throat, gentle but possessive, as I bring the other up, concealing the ring within it. I lick her swollen bottom lip, savoring her soft gasp.

"Now, you'll be mine in every conceivable way," I whisper, sliding the ring onto her finger. Her wide eyes tell me she understands. "Between the collar, the marks, this ring, and eventually our own family, there will never be any question that you belong to me."

I don't give her time to respond, pulling her closer to me by her hips. Reaching between us, I pinch her clit, sending her crashing over the edge. Her scream—*my name*—fills the air, her body shaking as her orgasm tears through her.

Her release triggers mine. I grind my teeth as the force of my climax overwhelms me. "Fuck, Anastasia," I groan, my voice ragged as I spill inside her.

When the waves of pleasure finally subside, I pull out slowly, savoring the soft whimpers that escape her lips. She lays back on the counter, her blonde hair spread out like a halo, her ivory skin marked with the evidence of my claim. My eyes drift to the new ring on her finger, the contrast of it against her flushed skin.

A sense of satisfaction settles over me. She *is* mine—in body, in soul, in every way that mattered.

I own her. Completely.

Epilogue

It's been six years since that Christmas when I got everything I ever wanted. A lot has changed since then. Damien and I got married three months after he made me his. We decided to wait until I graduated, even though we knew I'd be a stay-at-home mom. It just made sense to finish that semester and settle into married life before starting a family.

First, we welcomed a blond-haired, blue-eyed little boy, Aiden, followed by a brown-haired, brown-eyed little girl, Ruby, two years later. They're four and two now, and both are handfuls. Aiden may look like me, but he's his daddy's mini in every other way. And Ruby? She can rival my attitude on her worst days.

Some things, however, haven't changed. For instance, my husband still loves to lay claim to my body—just as he claimed every other part of my life. His need to own me, and my desire to be his, are precisely why I'm here, in this cabin, a week before Christmas… alone.

Every year, we come here. I always arrive first, enjoying a day or two alone with my books while Damien gives me the chance to decompress from the chaos of raising two toddlers.

When my phone buzzes, I know it's Damien. Taking the last sip of my peppermint hot chocolate, I open the message.

> I hope you enjoyed your hot chocolate. I know I will.

I glance at my now-empty cup and smile, already knowing what's to come. We've done this enough for me to recognize the signs—I have about ten minutes before the drug he slipped into my drink takes hold.

I head to the bedroom. I'll be asleep for most of this, but that doesn't stop me from preparing. I wouldn't mind being tied down, either, and the restraints are already in place on the bed in the back of the cabin.

Quickly, I change into a red thong and matching bra, feeling the first wave of drowsiness hit me. Crawling into bed, I cover myself with the blanket, keeping my eyes locked on the door. That's where he'll appear.

My eyelids grow heavy, the act of keeping them open becoming harder with each blink. Then, a figure appears in the doorway.

He's wearing all black and the same Krampus mask he wore that night all those years ago.

I struggle to keep my eyes open as he stalks across the room, his slow, deliberate movements filling me with anticipation. At the foot of the bed, he begins to undress.

"It looks like you're ready for me," he murmurs.

But before I can respond, sleep claims me.

***

I'm not sure how much time has passed, but the sensation of his mouth on my clit and his fingers curling inside me pulls me back into consciousness. A moan escapes my lips as he works me over with practiced precision.

Damien knows my body better than I do, and he knows how to coax pleasure from me—even in my sleep. I try to stay awake, to savor every second, but my eyes grow heavy again as his mouth trails up my body, leaving a path of marks in his wake.

***

The next time I wake, my wrists are restrained to the bed, my legs spread wide and held in place by a bar resting behind Damien's shoulders. He's pounding into me at a brutal, unrelenting pace, his bruising grip pressing me deeper into the mattress.

"Fuck," he groans, his voice rough. "Look at you, so ready for me even in your sleep."

My name falls from his lips as I feel the telltale build of an orgasm starting to take hold. A deep moan escapes me, catching his attention. He leans down, capturing my lips in a brief kiss before my body goes slack, and I'm dragged back into the dream world.

***

This time, I wake to a sharp sting on my clit. My eyes flutter open, and I see Damien kneeling beside my head. One hand strokes his cock, while the other toys with my sore, swollen pussy.

"Open your pretty little mouth," he demands.

I don't resist. His fingers work me closer to the edge as he slides his cock past my lips. The taste of me on him makes me moan, the vibrations traveling through him.

"Your pussy squeezed me so good," he growls, his thrusts growing faster and harder.

My eyes threaten to close again, but his voice keeps me tethered.

"Now, stay awake long enough to swallow every drop of my cum," he commands.

His words send a jolt of pleasure through me, making me gag slightly as he presses deeper. I don't want him to stop.

"Fuck, little angel, I'm going to cum."

He buries himself in my throat, his cock twitching as he releases. I swallow him down, savoring the way his entire body shudders in response.

Damien unties me quickly, pulling me into his arms and pressing a kiss to my hair.

"Such a good fucking slut for me," he murmurs.

A soft hum of satisfaction escapes me as I whisper, "I love you."

"I love you too, little angel," he replies, covering me with the blankets and settling beside me.

As I drift off again, completely spent, I feel utterly used and perfectly content in the way only my masked mystery man could ever provide.

Acknowledgements

First things first, thank you my wonderful, supportive husband who encouraged me to take this time to start writing. I never would have thought to use the time our kiddo is in school to work on writing my own books. And thank you for supporting me getting hyper-focused on this project and letting me bounce ideas off of you. I love you, Bo!!

A huge shout-out to my author friends, who have given me tips and offered encouraging words through this process. But the biggest shoutout goes to Nina Gia!! Thank you so much for everything you have done for me to help make this book possible. From helping me hone my brat skills for this book, to offering to edit for me, and everything in between! You are truly an amazing person, and friend. I cherish your advice, and input. This book seriously wouldn't be what it is without you! I love you girl!!

I also have to thank my friends who offered to beta-read my book, y'all are seriously amazing! It's a scary process to send something you created out into the world, but knowing you guys got it first, and how you all hype me up just makes it easier. I love you all!

Lilith Luxe did a phenomenal job with the front cover, she literally brought my vision to life!

I want to say thank you to every single one of my ARC members, and my street team. You guys make launch day possible, so thank you for all the feedback!! You guys are amazing!!

And lastly, thank you! My reader, thank you for taking a chance on my book. I hope it was everything you hoped it would be, and I hope you stay tuned for the next book!!

About the Author

Katie Night is a new romance author whose love for books led her on a new journey to write them.

Her love for books started over ten years ago. But it wasn't until she was a new mom who struggled to make like-minded friends, who were also on the same walk of life as herself for that love to flourish.

Over the last six years through all the ups and downs, she could always count on her husband, her family, and her books.

She had tried to write a couple of other books before, but it wasn't until she went out to dinner with two of her close friends that an idea blossomed and took off. That idea led to her very first book being published as the start of the Second Vow series, that book was just the beginning, her love for writing bloomed with that first book.

www.ingramcontent.com/pod-product-compliance
Lightning Source LLC
LaVergne TN
LVHW012017060526
838201LV00061B/4349